## MEMORIES

Tears pricked my eyelids. A silly song went buzzing round and round in my head. "Memories Are Made of This."

I had memories. Memories of a man standing in the rain beside a chess stall under the lime trees. Memories of a man who could be tender and gentle, strong and angry. Memories of a long goodnight kiss. Memories of a man who had shouted a frantic warning to me and saved my life. And then walked out of it!

Had his attentions been prompted only by duty? Would I ever see his handsome, smiling face again?

# SUDDENLY IT WAS LOVE

## *Daisy Thomson*

A JOVE/HBJ BOOK

First Jove/HBJ edition published December 1977

Library of Congress Catalog Card Number: 77-80709

Printed in the United States of America

Jove/HBJ books are published by Jove Publications, Inc.
(Harcourt Brace Jovanovich) 757 Third Avenue, New York,
N.Y. 10017

## Chapter 1

The dolls enchanted me. I watched with fascinated delight as the stout, drably clad woman, a cigarette dangling from the corner of her overlipsticked mouth, produced them one after another from an enormous suitcase. She arranged them on miniature deck chairs on a trestle table under the large striped umbrella she had erected to protect her wares from the downpour.

"Janey! Do come along!" muttered Sally impatiently. "You can see dolls like these anywhere. I want to spend the time ferreting around the famous Antique Market Under The Trees to see if I can pick up something unusual to take home with me."

"I think this student fringe, as they call this section of the market, will be every bit as interesting," I countered.

"Possiby," Sally agreed amiably, buttoning her raincoat up to the top of her neck. "On the other hand, it won't be quite so wet wandering under the canvas covers of the main stalls."

I continued to moon over the dolls, and said, "I tell you what. You go off and look at the things that you want specially to see, while I try to make up my mind if I can afford to buy one of these beguiling beauties! I shan't be long."

"You are an idiot, Janey," she sighed. "I bet they cost the earth, and old hatchet face who is selling them knows you are interested and will put up the price for you!"

"Sally! She might understand English!"

My friend shook her head. "I doubt it. In spite of what the guidebooks say, once you get away from the main shops and hotels, no one else in The Hague seems to be able to understand what I say." She shrugged. "Anyway, be careful, Janey. It would be silly to spend a great deal of money on the first day of the holiday. Remember, we have another ten to go!"

She sauntered off in the direction of the main line of stalls which were being set up for the famous Thursday open-air antique market in the Lange Verhout. The May-fresh green trees overhead made a pleasant setting for the weekly event, although the morning's unexpected rainstorm somewhat dampened the enthusiasm of visitors and potential buyers.

I turned my attention back to the dolls. They were beautifully made, with an eye to color and design which I could not associate with the untidy, overpowdered woman who was selling them.

There was one doll which I liked particularly. It had a pertly innocent face, with large blue

6

eyes and long gold hair, and the embroidered smile somehow managed to convey a sense of mischief and humor. It was dressed in a long blue-and-white gingham dress, and a white marguerite was tucked behind one ear. My little niece would love it, if I could bear to part with it—provided, of course, that I could afford to buy it.

As I continued to look at it, I knew that Sally would be right, as usual. A handmade doll like this, even if it was only a rag doll, would be ludicrously expensive, and from the way the woman was leering at me over the cigarette smoke which coiled from her lips, I guessed she realized my interest and would, as my friend had hinted, add several gulden to the price.

Reluctantly I turned away and went to study a line of strange-looking paintings which were pinned to a broad wooden board that rested against one of the lime trees. The paintings, and the small, insignificant-looking man who was sitting beside them, were sheltered from the rain by a kind of plastic tent top, which threatened to blow away with each fresh gust of wind.

After his first flickering glance in my direction, the artist ignored me and continued to sketch on the pad on his knee, while I stood looking at the strange products of his imagination.

Remembering the fresh innocence of the doll's pretty face, I found the scenes he had depicted doubly evil and loathsome. Black demons rode the wind to tilt at a white star with their blood-red spears. Headless serpents writhed among roofless, smoke-blackened houses. Satan flicked his forked tongue over a cradle where a child lay sleeping; but most disturbing of all was the painting of what appeared to be the face of a kindly old man. On closer inspection you saw that his left eye reflected all the most loathsome of sins, while the right eye was an upside-down ace of spades, with a grinning skull as its pupil. As I gaped at it, I had the strangest feeling that it had singled me out for its malevolent menace.

I stepped back with a shiver of unease, wanting to escape from the mesmeric gaze of the death's head as fast as I could, but as I turned hastily away I tripped over the feet of a young man who was sprawling on a low stool beside his own display of wares, which was set up between the revolting paintings and the dolls' stall.

I would have fallen on the slippery, leaf-wet ground if the man hadn't grabbed hold of me and held me firmly, so that for a few undignified seconds I lay spreadeagled across his denim-clad knees, before he gently helped to set me back on my feet.

"I am very sorry!" I spluttered in English. *"Het spijt me,"* I switched to Dutch. *"Ik ben u erg dankbaar!"*

"It's I that should be grateful!" The man grinned at me, his eyes, blue as the denim suit he was wearing, sparkling with amusement. "It isn't every day a pretty girl like you falls on my lap!"

8

I blushed, and the amusement in his eyes increased.

"I thought blushing went out with Queen Victoria," he teased, speaking in English. "How very nice to know that it didn't!"

I pulled myself away from his light clasp and tried to look dignified as I replied coldly:

"Thanks for helping me. I hope I didn't knock over any of your goods with my carelessness."

I glanced at his trestle table where, under a cellophane cover, a number of marquetry chessboards were set out. Some were in a plain frame, with only the squares for the game inlaid in different woods. Others were more ornate, with a variety of inlaid designs around the board—some had roses intertwined with fleur de lis, others were patterned with each man of the chess set, and others again were adorned with the signs of the zodiac.

"Do you make these boards?" I asked, my momentary indignation at his teasing forgotten in my admiration for his goods.

"I only wish I could." He shook his head regretfully. "These are the work of a friend. I am only standing in as salesman for him today."

"There is a lot of talent on display in this square today." I glanced involuntarily across at the doll stand, where I observed that a price list had been chalked up. These dolls cost much more than I had expected they might, and I sighed ruefully, knowing that it would be quite foolish to spend so much of my holiday allowance to gratify my childish desire to possess one.

"I was watching you looking at the doll counter a little earlier." The man followed my glance. "You seem fascinated by them."

"I think they are lovely! I had even considered buying one." I indicated my favorite in the blue-and-white gingham dress. "But not at that price! This is just the first day of my holiday, and with ten more days to think about, with meals and drinks and museums and things, I think I should forget about it." I sighed again.

"You know," the stranger cocked his head to one side and studied my face. "That particular doll looks rather like you."

I laughed. "Flattery will get you nowhere! I bet you say that to all the girls who stop by your stall, in order to try to persuade them to buy one of your friend's boards!" I glanced at his wares. "I take it that they will be even more expensive than the dolls?"

He nodded agreement. "They certainly are, but they are worth every cent."

"I hope you manage to sell a few."

"I hope so too. I have sold none so far, but the crowds don't start to arrive until later in the day, which is when business picks up."

We stood there, smiling at each other, both of us enjoying the unexpected conversational interlude.

Behind us, one of the stallholders from the antique side of the market was trying to remonstrate with a policeman, who was insisting that he move his car from the road where it was standing to the parking space cordoned off for dealers at the end of the square. Surely, he said, since his stall was only a few yards away and he had only a few more boxes to unload, surely, in view of the downpour, his waiting could be extended for another five minutes?

The policeman stolidly pointed out that he had already exceeded his allotted time by a quarter of an hour, and he must now remove his car without further delay.

The chessboard seller grinned at me, and remarked, "Police and traffic wardens are the same the world over, aren't they?" He seemed as reluctant to end the interlude as I was.

"Don't be too hard on them," I replied amiably. "They only do the job they have been given to do."

As I finished speaking, Sally came hurrying across the rain-swept space between the fringe stalls and the main ones.

"Janey!" she scolded as she came up to me. "What's been keeping you? I've been waiting and waiting for you to join me!"

As she addressed me, I was aware that the man beside me was looking at her in the interested manner in which most men tend to look at Sally.

In spite of the wind and the rain, she managed to look trim and elegant in her white, belted raincoat, her dark hair tucked almost completely out of sight under a navy scarf tied pirate-fashion round her head, exposing only the lobes of her tiny ears with their glowing, pearl stud earrings. This severe style emphasized the perfection of her features and the creamy smoothness of her skin.

In contrast, I was unhappily aware that I must look very ordinary in my shapeless yellow anorak with its equally shapeless hood slipping back from my fair hair.

In her impatience, Sally grabbed me by the arm.

"Janey, do come along!" she exhorted me. "I have just seen an interesting-looking door knocker to add to my collection," she went on, as she dragged me back in the direction from which she had come, in her excitement quite oblivious to the fact that she had rudely interrupted my chat with the good-looking stall-holder.

"Oh, Janey! It's, it's—" Words failed her for the moment as she continued to propel me forward. "It's so different! It's quaint and unusual and," her eyes gleamed with delight, "it is actually quite cheap, but—" She continued to talk, but I wasn't listening to her.

I was feeling rather peeved at the way she had interrupted my conversation, although conversation was perhaps too grand a way to describe what had been little more than a pleasant passing of the time of day between two strangers. I was equally peeved at the way she had dragged me off without giving me a chance to say a polite goodbye.

I pulled myself free of her restraining grip and

turned around. The man was staring after us, so I raised my hand in a friendly farewell gesture.

"I hope for your friend's sake you get a few customers, in spite of the rain!" I called back to him.

Sally, her flow of words halted by my action, stopped short and turned to gape, first at me and then back at the stranger who was returning my salute.

"Janey! Who on earth is that?" she demanded.

"One of the fringe stallholders," I informed her, smiling. "We met when I accidentally tripped over his feet, and he managed to save me from falling. Somehow we got into conversation. He speaks very good English."

"What you mean is that he went out of his way to chat you up in order to try to sell you something!" sniffed Sally knowingly.

My glow of pleasure from the encounter faded as I muttered, "I'm sure that wasn't what he had in mind! I think he merely wanted to have a chat in English. In any case," I cheered up again at the thought, "he knew I couldn't afford to buy one of his expensive chessboards any more than I could afford to buy that doll I coveted. Do you know how much it cost?" I turned to her, wide-eyed, and mentioned the sum.

"As much as that?" grimaced Sally. "What a shame! You had set your heart on it, hadn't you?"

"Tell me more about this door knocker of

yours." I switched the subject. "If you like it, and it is so cheap, why didn't you buy it?"

"I tried to, but the stupid girl behind the counter couldn't understand English and didn't even try to understand my sign language, when I pointed to it and to the money in my hand to indicate that I wanted to buy it. She merely gaped at me as if she thought I had gone mad!

"I stood at the stall waiting for you to arrive, but when you didn't show up, I decided to come and fetch you."

Sally was walking so quickly I could hardly keep pace with her long strides.

"I do hope she hasn't sold it in the interval," she muttered. "These assistants often keep back bargains for their friends!"

To Sally's relief, the object she coveted still lay among a jumble of other bric-a-brac which had not yet been sorted out on a table at the back of the stall. To me, it didn't look very prepossessing. It was a dirt-ingrained, verdigrised gadget in the shape of a dragon some nine inches long and about five inches at its broadest part. One of the half-folded wings was dented, and it was almost impossible to make out any markings on the body because of the layers of grime.

"What do you think?" Sally beamed at me. "Isn't it lovely! It will take pride of place in my collection!"

"It looks as if it has just been dragged from the bottom of a sewer!" I said tactlessly. "You would think the stallholder would at least have tried to clean it up a little!"

14

"Dealers in this kind of thing haven't the time to clean up everything they get hold of," snapped Sally. "Now, go ahead," she nudged me forward. "You explain to the girl you want to buy it. Here is the money—eight gulden—you can see the price marked on it from here."

"Sally, I am sure it isn't worth even four gulden!" I glanced again at the shoddy-looking object.

"Please, Janey," she pleaded. "I want it. If you don't like practicing your Dutch while I am within earshot, I'll go across to the stall over there and look at the old photograph albums!"

I shrugged and took the money from her. If she wanted to throw a couple of pounds away on a piece of old junk, well, that was her business!

I leaned over the counter to attract the attention of the sullen-faced young woman who lurked in the shadows at the back of the stall. She glowered at me, and at first made no attempt to serve me.

"*Ik wil dat kopen!*" I said firmly, pointing to the dragon on the table beside her.

"*Dit?*" She looked down at the tray of junk and picked up the knocker, at the same time glancing at her watch.

"*Ja!*" I nodded.

She looked down at it and shrugged as if she didn't think much of my choice, before coming forward and handing it to me to let me examine it.

"*Dank u!*" I said, trying not to let my own

15

distaste for the grimy object show as I pretend-
ed to study it.

Although I guessed it might look a little more
attractive if it was cleaned and polished, even
close at hand it didn't appeal to me. In its
present state, and with its dented wing, I felt it
was grossly overpriced at eight gulden, but if
Sally was keen to have it, the price was no
concern of mine.

"I'll take it!" I handed the money Sally had
given me to the assistant.

Still unsmiling, she took it from me and
dropped it into an old tin box under a table at
the back of the stall, pulled a crumpled piece of
newspaper from another box, and carelessly
wrapped up the dragon, which she returned to
me before once again retreating sullenly to the
shadows at the back of her stall.

I hurried back to the spot where I had left
Sally, but as I drew near to the booth where she
had been looking at some old postcards, a blus-
tery gust of wind whipped back the end of the
canvas overstructure, and a spray of water was
dashed into my eyes, half blinding me. I went
forward to tap the white-coated woman, who
was leaning over the counter examining the mer-
chandise, on the shoulder.

"I managed to get the dragon, in spite of the
unhelpful assistant who will never make it as
saleswoman of this or any other year!" I said.

The woman swung round, and although her
face was vaguely familiar, it wasn't Sally's face.

"I'm sorry!" I spluttered. "I thought you were

a friend of mine. You are wearing the same color of waterproof—"

The woman gave me a frigid glance and turned away to study the postcards she had been viewing before I distracted her attention.

I felt about the size of a half-penny as I walked away from her and looked around to see where Sally had got to.

I found her a couple of stalls further on, poking about another tray of junk.

"There's your dragon." I handed her the untidy parcel.

"You got it!" she exclaimed, smiling gratefully.

"Just!" I brushed the rain from my face. "As you remarked, the girl at the stall was a bit dumb."

Sally took the packet from me, grimaced at the careless way in which it had been wrapped, and removed the crumpled paper from it. Opening her smart, brief-case-styled handbag, she withdrew the large square envelope which held the maps and guidebooks the travel agency had supplied us with, and carefully placed the knocker among the circulars before restoring the envelope to her tidy bag.

"I don't know how to thank you, Janey. I did so want this dragon, but that silly girl just wouldn't sell it to me. Oh!" she sighed happily, "I can hardly wait to get back to the hotel to start cleaning it up!"

We walked up the lane of stalls and back down the other side, repassing en route the bric-a-brac stall. The grumpy girl who had sold me the dragon with such ill grace was being angrily rated by the man who had argued with the police about parking his car, but I doubted if anything he said would penetrate the thick skin of his dour assistant.

In spite of the range of goods we looked at, I saw nothing which appealed to me as much as the lovely doll I had set my sights on, or as the marquetry chessboards my friendly salesman had shown me.

On our return journey to the hotel, we had to pass the doll stall, and I went to have another look at what I called "my doll." To my disappointment, it had gone. In its place was an equally cute model—a pert young girl in jeans, with an enormous red apple appliqued on the bib front. Her yellow hair was screwed into two tight, sticky-out pigtails tied with blue ribbon, and in fact, the jeans with the scarlet apple on the bib top, the pigtailed hair, and the mischievous expression could have been modeled from my own niece.

"Sally! Look! Isn't that Elspeth to the life? Oh, I simply must buy it for her!"

"Janey, it's ridiculously expensive!"

"I know." I was not to be deterred. "But just think how Elspeth would love it. It will be worth doing without a few lunches, just to see her face."

The woman with the cigarette drooping from her mouth was not in evidence, and it was a cheerful-faced teenager who slipped the doll into a plastic bag for me after I had counted out my money.

As I carefully folded my parcel and placed it into my capacious shoulder bag to keep it dry, I glanced across at the chessboard counter, hoping to be able to indicate to the pleasant young man that I had bought a doll after all, but he was standing with his back to me, deep in conversation with a short, broad-shouldered man in a navy raincoat. He didn't notice me.

I felt an odd sensation of disappointment. We had spoken to each other for only a few minutes, and yet I felt as if we were old friends and would have liked to say hello to him once again.

The rain, which had stopped for a short time, started up again and became heavier and heavier, while thunder grumbled menacingly overhead.

"We shall be soaked to the skin by the time we get to Molen Straat!" moaned Sally. "Let's make a dash for the road on the south side of the square. We might be able to flag down a taxi."

The fresh young leaves, stripped from the trees by the gale, were wet and slippery under our feet as we hurried through the park to the roadside. We stopped at the curb to let a stream of traffic go past, and as we stood under the dripping branches of the limes, waiting for an opportunity to cross, I heard the sound of footsteps running toward us.

With an absurd feeling of happiness, I thought it might be my young man, who could have noticed me after we had passed his stand, and was wanting to say hello again.

I glanced over my shoulder just as a young fellow, with a balaclava-style woolen cap pulled down over his forehead and the lower part of his face completely hidden by the turned-up collar of his jacket, lunged at us, pushing us roughly forward into the street.

As we stumbled over the curb, he made a swift grab at my bag. I had twined its long leather shoulder strap round and round my wrist as a normal safety precaution, and as the youth pulled wildly at the bag, a sharp pain shot up my arm as the thong tightened over the flesh and bone at the base of my hand. The strong yank on the bag prevented me from falling into the roadway as Sally had done, and as I struggled to keep on my feet, I called out in anger and dismay.

A passer-by on the opposite pavement glanced over to see what was happening, and as the lad persisted in trying to get possession of the bag, he let out a shout and came running to my assistance, while Sally, who had scrambled to her feet, screamed, "Help! Help! Police! Stop, thief!"

With the shouting, the agonizing wrenching on my wrist stopped and the young man darted off, empty-handed, through the trees, zigzagging in and out between the trunks until he was lost to view behind the first of the market stalls.

## Chapter 2

A small crowd of curious people gathered round us, wanting to know what had happened, and within half a minute a gray-uniformed policeman came marching across the square to demand what the commotion was about.

I tried to explain, but with excitement, my fluency in Dutch vanished, and I stumbled through my recital half in English, while the man who had come to our help kept interrupting me to give the policeman his version of the affair.

The officer told him he would hear his story later, and insisted on my starting mine right from the beginning again. By this time both Sally and I were shivering with cold and nerves, and wondering how much longer we would be kept standing in the pouring rain while the policeman continued to question us. I was about to ask the man if we couldn't go and stand under cover, when from behind me I heard a voice I recognized call out something to the officer.

He turned, as both Sally and I did, and I

sighed with profound relief when I saw the tow-headed man from the chessboard stall insinuate his way through the rubber-neckers to come and stand beside us.

"What is all the excitement?" he asked me in English.

"A young thug came running up behind us, pushed us off the pavement and tried to steal my shoulder bag!" I said shakily. "He almost broke my wrist in the process," I added, pushing back my sleeve and gingerly easing loose the leather thong which was still cutting into my skin.

Sally and the policeman gasped when they saw the deep, ugly weal it had made, and the man's mouth tightened in anger as he too looked down and saw how the force of my assailant's pull on the bag had made the strap cut through the skin, so that a line of tiny blood bubbles oozed from it.

"Tell me quickly what happened," he ordered. "I shall translate for the officer's benefit, and then we shall go and get that wrist of yours attended to."

"It will be all right once I run cold water over it and clean it with antiseptic." I made light of my injury as I slipped the shoulder bag over my other arm and let the anorak sleeve fall back over my wrist to hide the disfiguring mark, but I could not control an involuntary wince as the cold, damp material brushed against the tender flesh.

The stallholder fluently translated what I had

to say to the policeman, who then asked if I would recognize the youth again if I saw him.

I hesitated. "I don't know. His face was so covered up that all I could distinguish were his eyes." I shivered. "They were dark, staring, with pinpoint pupils."

I stopped, although I had the feeling that I had overlooked something as the policeman filled in these details before turning to our rescuer to put a few questions to him. Before he could do so, the tow-headed man took him aside and said something to him in a low voice. The policeman listened attentively, nodded, snapped his notebook shut and turned once more to Sally and me, to tell us that we could go. He had our names and knew where we were staying, and if there were any further developments he would let us know. With that, he saluted and walked away.

Upon his going, the small crowd which had gathered quickly dispersed, and only the man in the blue denim suit remained with us.

He smiled his friendly smile.

"What you two young women need," he decided, "is a cup of strong black coffee, with perhaps a dash of something in it to heat you up."

He stepped between us, and taking each of us by an arm, he steered us across the road to the Pulchri Taveerne, which was only a few yards further up the street.

"What I could do with," said Sally, still shivering as she clung to his arm, "is a good hot bath and a change of clothes. Just look at the hem of my coat! It's filthy after stumbling to my knees when that little rat shoved me over."

"It isn't as bad as all that," the man chaffed her, smiling at her in a way which made me flush with uncalled-for irritation. "You can leave your wet coat in the cloakroom while we go to the restaurant, and when it is dry the dirt will rub off easily."

Sally responded to the charm of his smile as I had responded earlier.

"I hope this place doesn't cost the earth!" she pouted, raising no further demur about the wetness of her clothes as we entered the attractive hallway leading to the restaurant. "Janey and I have already spent more than we intended to today."

"Before we proceed further—" The man stopped in the foyer, and this time he turned to smile at me. "I think we should introduce ourselves. I am Dirk van der Woude."

"I'm Sally MacAdam."

"I'm Janey Mathieson."

We solemnly shook hands, although I could not help wincing when a spasm of pain shot up my arm as Dirk took hold of my hand.

He frowned.

"Let me have another look at your wrist," he said, continuing to hold my hand, while with the fingers of his left hand he gently turned back the cuff of my anorak.

"It looks very painful." He shook his head. "I think you should have it seen to."

"It will be all right," I muttered, my cheeks

flushing with embarrassment as he continued to hold my hand and stare down at the weals around my wrist. "I shall go to the Dames right away, give it a wash, smooth on some antiseptic cream and cover it with a plaster. I shan't be long."

Van der Woude raised his eyebrows in an inquiring look, and Sally chuckled as she explained.

"Janey's a nurse. She always carries a compact first-aid kit in that bag of hers."

"Ah!" he nodded. "Good. While you two go off to the Dames to see to Janey's wrist, I shall book a table for us."

Sally glanced at him with surprise.

"Don't tell me you have to reserve a table here just for a coffee!"

He shook his head with a smile.

"You may not have realized it, but it is after one o'clock," he indicated the time on his watch. "I was hoping, if you haven't made a previous arrangement, that you would join me for lunch here? It is a very good restaurant—real old Dutch. I am sure you will enjoy both the food and the atmosphere."

"I am not very hungry," I said hurriedly, knowing that after my extravagant purchase of the doll for my niece I could not have much more than the price of a coffee left in my purse that morning.

"I am!" said Sally firmly. "It is ages since we had breakfast, and we didn't have our usual morning coffee. Come along, Janey." She touched my arm. "We shall go and make ourselves presentable again, while Dirk sweet-talks the headwaiter into giving us a table at the window, with a view over the park!" She turned to our companion with her most beguiling look.

"We shan't be long," she promised.

"Sally!" I protested with annoyance once we were out of van der Woude's hearing. "You shouldn't have said yes. You know I won't be able to afford to lunch in a place like this, after what I spent this morning. I am sure it will be very expensive. It has that look," I added in a worried tone.

"Don't be silly!" she scolded. "You have to eat somewhere, and I can lend you some money if you are short. In any case," she went on, a smile tugging at her lips, "I wasn't going to be silly and turn down Dirk's invitation. I rather like him, and it would be fun to have a pleasant young man in tow from time to time, while we are on holiday here."

She pushed open the door marked "Dames" and ushered me into the ladies' room.

"Even in these days of sex equality, there is something to be said for having a man around, especially a dishy man like our new Dutch friend!"

I crossed over to a washbasin to run water over my wrist, and it wasn't the pain of the grazed and bruised skin which made me pout unhappily at myself in the mirror behind the basin. It was the knowledge that history was about to repeat itself, for over and over again, in the years since childhood that Sally and I had been friends, she had unwittingly beguiled the men who attracted me, away from me, and today it was plain that she found van der Woude every bit as charming as I had done and intended to flirt with him.

While I attended to my wrist, Sally took off her waterproof, untied the scarf which covered her head, and skillfully set about freshening her makeup.

I studied her reflection covertly in the mirror as she carefully combed her hair, admiring the way it fell perfectly into place. It had been feather-cut by an expert to make the most of the neat shape of her head and her long, slender neck.

I tried not to feel envious as I looked at her. In Sally's job as a TV interviewer and announcer, she was expected to look composed and elegant at all times, and over the years she had learned how to make the most of herself.

She applied a deep red lipstick to her mouth with practiced strokes, dusted the minimum of powder on nose and cheeks to tone down the glow of her complexion without dulling it, and then, satisfied with the result, she replaced her makeup kit in her handbag, stood up and studied herself in the full-length mirror at the opposite end of the room.

I dragged a comb hurriedly through my shoulder-length, light-brown hair. It had been soaked by the rain when my anorak hood had slipped off during my struggle with the would-be bag snatcher, and in spite of my efforts, it hung down limply, giving me a woebegone look.

"Hurry, Janey, or Dirk will get impatient," entreated Sally, eager to be off. "You look fine! That brandy-colored suit you are wearing was a clever buy. It emphasizes your peachy complexion." She tried to boost my morale as she led the way back to the foyer where van der Woude was waiting for us.

A waiter directed us to a table beside one of the windows and handed us menu cards as we sat down.

It was not so much the food list as the price list which I was interested in. I wanted to know if there was a minimum charge, and I drew a quiet breath of relief when I worked out that I did have enough money left over, after my extravagance of the morning, to pay for a meal if I chose the least expensive item.

Dirk was the first to decide what he wanted to order.

"I can recommend the bacon pancakes," he told us. "That's what I'm going to have—and a beer to go with it. How about you, Sally?"

"What is this item—*uitsmijter?*" she asked. "It sounds exotic, but it is reasonably priced, and Janey and I have to be careful how we eke out our money. We don't want to be completely broke before the end of our holiday!"

"*Uitsmijter?*" repeated Dirk with a smile. "It is not quite as exotic as it may sound to you. It is actually bacon and eggs on top of a piece of bread."

"Then I shall have it!" Sally smiled back at him.

"How about you, Janey?" Van der Woude turned to me.

"Like you, I shall have a bacon pancake, but with a cup of coffee instead of beer."

"Is this your first visit to Holland?" Dirk inquired after he had given our order to the waiter.

"No," Sally shook her head. "I spent a few days in Amsterdam, at a conference, last year, but I did not have time to do much sightseeing. However, what I did see made me eager to come back again for a holiday, if I ever had the opportunity."

"And now you have had the opportunity?" He continued to look at her with interest. "Are you glad you came?"

"Definitely!" Her eyes twinkled at him. "I think I am going to enjoy myself even more than I expected to do. Actually," she turned to me to include me in the conversation, "it is Janey who is responsible for our coming here just now. Her brother is getting married on Saturday to a Dutch girl, who lives in a small village about a couple of hours' drive from The Hague, and naturally she wanted to attend his wedding. As a friend of the family, I was invited as well, and we worked out that the cheapest way to manage was to come with a package tour, which meant we could combine our holiday with Tim's big day."

"So you and I will both have a Dutch connection?" Dirk looked at me. "My grandfather is Dutch, although he spent the greater part of his life in Scotland, where I was born."

"I thought you were a Hollander," I said in astonishment, "and," I uttered a giggle, "I was admiring your fluent command of our language!"

"I'm bilingual," he explained. "I still have relatives in Holland, and I visit the country as often as possible."

"Janey speaks some Dutch too!" said Sally proudly.

"Only a few words," I intervened hastily, mindful of the fiasco of my recent interview with the policeman. "I took a crash course in the language when Tim told me he intended marrying Anna. I thought it might be nice for her if there was someone else in the family she could talk to in her own language. Then," I grimaced, "Tim mentioned that his bride-to-be speaks fluent English, and in fact, is a part-time English teacher at the local school, when she isn't helping on the farm."

"At least your efforts weren't in vain," Sally encouraged me. "If you hadn't been able to talk some Dutch, I would never have got hold of the door knocker I wanted!"

Sally went on to explain to van der Woude about her collection of old knockers, which included items from every foreign city she had visited, and to tell him about the difficulty she had had in trying to buy her latest acquisition. While she talked, I glanced with interest around the charming Dutch restaurant.

Most of the tables were now occupied, and from the snatches of conversation I overheard, many of the diners were visitors who had been visiting the market in the square across from the Pulchri. The woman I had mistaken for Sally at the postcard stall was sitting at a table near the door with a group of people, some of whose faces were familiar to me from a TV serial I had followed during the winter months.

"Sally!" I attracted my friend's attention away from the man on whom she was unblinkingly focusing her witch-green eyes. "Remember I told you I mistook another woman for you in the market? She is over there, at that table beside the door, with a crowd of TV actors. I am sure I should know who she is, but I can't put a name to her."

Sally glanced casually in the direction I had indicated.

"That's Natasha Berg," she told me. "She is an ex-beauty queen. Miss Rose of England, or something like that. It wasn't one of the big beauty events, but it landed her a contract advertising soaps and toothpastes on TV. Then she married a Swiss millionaire, almost old enough to be her grandfather. He appears to be crazy about her, and backed her in a couple of West End plays which flopped. Finally she made it in a small part in a TV series last year, once again, according to gossip, because her husband used his not inconsiderable influence!"

As if she sensed that we were discussing her, Natasha Berg glanced across at our table. Her eyes flickered from me to Sally, and it was on Sally, not me, that her speculative gaze rested for a second or two. No doubt she recognized my friend since they worked in the same medium, and she might be wondering if Sally was in The Hague in connection with her work.

Meanwhile, Dirk was looking at my friend with frowning interest.

"How come you know so much about Natasha Berg?" he demanded. "You don't happen to be a journalist, do you?"

"I do do some free-lance writing." She nodded. "However, my main line is radio and TV interviewing, which means I have to keep up with people who get into the limelight from time to time, and how Natasha loves to be in the limelight!" She shook her head. "Apart from publicity, that young woman has only two loves in her life—clothes and money—and more money!"

"That makes three other loves, not two!" grinned Dirk. "You make her seem like a certain Greek's widow, and come to that," he glanced across at the woman under discussion, "she isn't unlike that lady in looks."

He sipped at his beer and studied Sally over the rim of his glass.

"I ought to have recognized you, Sally, when you introduced yourself. Although I myself have never watched your interviews on the small screen, my sister is a great admirer of yours, and constantly talks about 'Sally MacAdam's hairstyles' and 'Sally MacAdam's clothes', and the way Sally MacAdam cuts young would-be's down to size!"

He reconsidered her with admiration as he added, "She is going to be envious when I tell her that I had lunch with you."

Sally looked pleased, although she brushed aside his flattery by saying, "I interview celebrities, Dirk, but I am not one myself, and I don't expect to be recognized by the public."

We chatted for another ten minutes or so, and then Dirk signaled to the waiter to bring the bill.

I opened my bag to get out my change purse, but had some difficulty in finding it because of the parcel which took up most of the space.

Dirk watched with amusement as I groped around.

"What on earth do you carry in that hold-all of yours, apart from first-aid kits and the like?" he teased.

"This!" I beamed at him, pulling out the packet. "I forgot to tell you, I bought a rag doll after all!"

"I knew you wouldn't be able to resist it!" He grinned triumphantly. "That was why I told the woman at the stall to set your gingham girl aside for you. I was afraid someone else might buy it before you came back."

"Oh, no!" I gasped. "When we returned to the stall and I couldn't see it, I bought another doll, almost, but not quite, as attractive. Look!" I pulled the pigtailed cutie from its bag.

Van der Woude looked disappointed as he took the doll from me and, oblivious of the amused stares of the diners at the next table, held it up to examine it.

"Yes, this one is quite attractive too," he agreed, "but it is not a patch on the charmer with the marguerite in her hair!"

He shook his head. "I can't understand why Rosa didn't produce it for you. When I described you to her, she recognized you immediately, and promised she would keep a look out for your return."

"It was a young girl who sold me the doll—"

"Never mind," Sally intervened. "I like the one you have there, and your young niece will too, and that's the main thing."

I replaced my purchase carefully in its container and folded it into my bag once again, as the waiter came over to the table to present the bill. In spite of Dirk's protests, Sally and I handed him our share of the payment.

"Since we are in Holland," I pointed out to him with a smile, "it is fitting that we should go Dutch!"

On our way from the dining room we had to pass the table where Natasha Berg was sitting. Natasha did not deign to look our way, but one of her companions called out a hello to Sally, and asked her if she had come to The Hague to do a report on the new thriller series he and his team were making.

She shook her head. "I'm here on holiday," she told him.

"Where are you staying?" asked the rugged-faced actor, who invariably plays the role of a rough, tough detective. "I might look you up and drag you out for a meal some night." He leered at her. "That is, if I can find the time to spare."

"We are the ones who won't have any time to spare," Sally replied coolly. "We have a very full program arranged for our holiday!"

She bade him a polite goodbye and followed Dirk and me to the foyer.

Dirk looked at him quizzically.

"I know a number of young women who would have accepted an invitation to dine with Saunders with alacrity!"

Sally shrugged. "I daresay some women find him attractive, but he isn't my type. His manners are the same off the screen as on it, and rudeness and discourtesy have no appeal for me."

Dirk helped us into our coats and we walked down the steps from the Pulchri entrance into the tree-lined street.

The rain had stopped and the sun was blinking hopefully through the thinning gray clouds as we set off for our hotel.

To my surprise, van der Woude accompanied us along the road, chatting amiably with Sally, telling her the places we ought to visit and also recommending the names of some inexpensive restaurants where, he said, we would get good value for our money.

We came to the junction at Noord Einde, and were about to turn into Molen Straat when I felt the hairs at the nape of my neck stand up with nervous foreboding. I clutched at Dirk's arm.

"What's wrong?" He glanced at me, puzzled.

"Look! Over there!" I pointed across the street. "Going into the stationer's shop. I am almost certain that is the youngster who tried to snatch my bag this morning."

Dirk turned around and stared in the direction I was indicating.

"Janey, are you sure?"

"He is dressed in exactly the same way, and—"

"Really, Janey!" interrupted Sally. "Half the teenagers I have seen in The Hague sport tattered jeans and woolen balaclavas! It's the current fashion of their age group."

Dirk nodded agreement, saying, "Apart from that, I very much doubt if your young scoundrel would hang about this district, knowing the police are on the look-out for him, and knowing, too, that the pair of you got a good look at him this morning and would not hesitate to call the nearest officer if you spotted him again."

I bit my lip.

"I still think it was the same lad!" I persisted. "I had one of my feelings, rather like a sixth sense, which made me think that someone was watching me. I looked over the road, and there he was, skulking in that doorway. He hurried inside when he saw that I had spotted him."

"For goodness sake!" Sally laughed and shook her head as she turned to Dirk. "Janey is always having these feelings," she chuckled. "It is something to do with her Highland ancestry! But she is not always right, and in this particular case, I think she has let her nerves get the better of her.

"Now Janey," she spoke more seriously as she addressed me, "I am not going to have you jumping at shadows for the rest of the holiday! Get it into that imaginative little head of yours that it could not possibly have been the same boy, for the very good reasons Dirk has pointed out.

"In any case," she teased me, "aren't you rather flattering yourself? Why should a thief follow you around, when there are plenty of wealthier-looking women in the town to steal from?"

Instinct can't argue against logic. Instinct told me that I was right, and it was the bag snatcher I had seen. Logic, as expressed by both Dirk and Sally, seemed to refute the fact.

I knew better than to continue the argument, and in this case, I fervently hoped that my friends were right.

I shrugged to indicate my agreement, and Sally slipped her arm through van der Woude's and nudged him to continue on our way, but Dirk, as if he sensed I was still feeling uneasy, in turn took hold of my arm, giving it a reassuring squeeze as he did so. So arm in arm, like old friends, the three of us strolled along the street to the hotel where Sally and I were staying.

*Chapter 3*

We stopped outside the entrance to the Hotel Collenius. Van der Woude looked up at the long rectangle of blue sky above the narrow street and remarked cheerfully, "It would seem that the sun is going to shine for you, for a few hours at least, this afternoon. That will make it much pleasanter for wandering round the town on your sightseeing tour."

"Are you returning to your market stall?" I asked. "I feel guilty at keeping you away from it for so long."

"That's all right!" Dirk's smile was for both of us. "As I told you, another friend had taken over for the lunch hour shift shortly before I came over to find what trouble you had got into with the local police. I only hope he has managed to sell a few more of the boards than I did."

"I wish I had been able to afford to buy one for my father." I shook my head. "They were most attractive."

"But you preferred spending your money on

38

the doll with the pigtails!" he chaffed me. "So much for my salesmanship."

"Dirk, it was very kind of you to take us under your wing the way you did," butted in Sally, who never liked to be left out of a conversation. "We did appreciate it!"

"I enjoyed having the excuse to have lunch with two very pretty strangers," he twinkled at her. "It isn't every day I have such good fortune, and my friends will be envious when I tell them about it."

From a nearby steeple a clock chimed, indicating that it was half past two o'clock.

Van der Woude glanced down at his own watch to confirm the time.

"I hadn't realized that it was so late!" he exclaimed. "The time seems to have flown past! I'm afraid I shall have to leave you." He smiled ruefully. "If I don't put in an appearance at the market soon, Jan will think I have walked out on him.

"Have a good time this evening," he smiled, referring to the fact that Sally had told him earlier that my brother, his bride-to-be, and Mike Russell, his best man, were coming to visit us in our hotel in the evening. "And thanks for a very pleasant luncheon break!"

He made no suggestion that we should meet again as he wished us goodbye, and as he went striding swiftly back down Molen Straat, both Sally and I gazed after him with a disappointed look in our eyes.

"Come along, Janey!" snapped Sally impatiently when he had disappeared from view around the corner. "I want to get to my room and have a bath and change into something fresh." She glanced down with a look of disgust at the oily marks which, in spite of her recent efforts in the powder room at the Pulchri, still soiled the hem of her coat.

She turned abruptly and pushed open the swing door of the hotel, adding in a less impatient tone, "Truth to tell, I am dying to have a good look at my little dragon." She patted her handbag. "I have an idea he is more in need of a bath than I am."

We retrieved our keys from the receptionist and took the lift up to the second floor. Although our bedrooms were in the same corridor, and overlooked a pretty park at the back of the hotel, Sally's room was beside the lift, while mine was at the far end of the passage. Next to it was a long, narrow window from which a fire escape ladder led to a narrow cat walk which bridged the space between the Hotel Collenius and the flat roof of the annex across a narrow lane.

Before we parted company, Sally suggested that in an hour's time we should go for a stroll around the town, to familiarize ourselves with the streets in the vicinity so that we shouldn't lose ourselves, as we had done the previous year when we had spent our holiday in Paris.

I had just stepped from the shower, which was in a cubicle beside the bedroom door, when the telephone rang.

Hastily wrapping the towel around me, I hurried to the bedside table and lifted up the receiver. My first, elated thought had been that Dirk van der Woude, realizing he had made no plan to meet us again, was telephoning to suggest a further meeting. I experienced the faintest sensation of disappointment when I recognized my brother Tim's voice as he said:

"Janey? Is that you? Welcome to Holland!"

He went on to say that he was calling to tell me that unfortunately Anna, his bride-to-be, would not, after all, be able to come with him to The Hague that evening. There had been some mix-up about her wedding dress, and she would have to wait at home for another fitting. She was extremely sorry about the contretemps, as she had been looking forward to meeting me for the first time, and now this would not be until her wedding day.

However, Tim went on, since Anna wasn't coming with him, it meant that he and Mike Russell, who was also attending the College in Bolsward, the town near which Anna lived, would be able to come to The Hague a couple of hours earlier than previously arranged, if that didn't interfere with any plans Sally and I had already made.

"I am looking forward to having a good talk with you, Janey!" he went on before I could reply. "It has been a long time since we have seen each other, and there will be a lot of family news to catch up on. Perhaps it is just as well that Anna can't manage tonight, or she might

41

have felt a bit left out of things while we chatted about people and events which for the time being would mean nothing to her."

"I'll fall in with your change of plans, on one condition," I told him.

"What's that?" he asked warily.

"That you take Sally and me out for an Indonesian meal! We have been told we ought to sample one while we are here."

"And so you shall!" replied Tim cheerfully. "Mike and I are both *Rijstafel* addicts, and I am sure you will be too, once you have sampled Indonesian food! See you later, then, Janey!" he said, and hung up.

I got in touch with Sally on the interroom phone service to tell her of Tim's call, and the change of plans.

"I'm sorry Anna can't manage, but I am delighted the boys are coming so early! I expect they know their way about The Hague, so they can come with us on the stroll we planned and tell us what places we should see and what streets we ought not to stroll down on our own at nights!"

She surprised me by giving a nervous giggle and adding, "I have been thinking over this morning's unpleasant episode, and I didn't realize how much it had upset me. The thought of having two stalwarts like Tim and Mike to escort us on our evening walk is very comforting! What time are they arriving?"

"Tim said they were leaving Bolsward almost immediately, and that it takes about two and a

42

half hours to reach The Hague by car, give or take ten minutes dependent on weather and traffic conditions."

"That should give you plenty of time to make yourself pretty for Mike!" teased Sally.

"The same goes for you!" I retorted briskly. "In fact, more so! I have a shrewd idea Mike has a soft spot for you. He asks after you each time I see him."

"Don't be silly, Janey." She laughed at the idea. "Everyone knows he haunted Gartlands when you were at home."

"It was Tim he came to see. Not me."

"You underestimate yourself, Janey." Sally's tone was surprisingly serious. "You shouldn't, you know. Instead of hovering around in the background of parties, as you invariably do, you should come forward and make the most of yourself. I know you like Mike, so let him become aware of you as a person in your own right, and not just his friend Tim's little sister."

I did not take her up on this statement. Sally is constantly on at me to develop a more positive personality. She thinks I am too gentle, too inclined to let myself be imposed on, too inclined to listen to other people instead of taking part in a conversation. She does not realize that I am happy to be as I am, and that I would find it embarrassing to adopt a more aggressive pose and push myself into the limelight.

As for making Mike notice me, I giggled to myself. Mike noticed me all right, when he wanted someone to darn his clothes or do some ironing, or a shoulder to cry on when his love life was in ruins, as he put it—an event which occurred with monthly regularity. In short, Mike Russell looked on me as a sister, and because we had lived on neighboring farms most of our lives, and had grown up together, I regarded him like a member of my own family—a kind of adopted brother. He was certainly not someone I wanted to provoke to a passing flirtation.

"You are quite wrong about Mike's interest in me, Sally." I refuted the suggestion once again. "I am not pulling your leg when I tell you that he was never able to keep his eyes off you when you came to spend a holiday at Gartlands. Come to think of it," I added mischievously, "he once told me he much preferred brunettes to blondes, so be careful!"

There was a short silence while Sally considered this information, until I said:

"Since we shan't be going out for our walk for another couple of hours, I think I shall have a rest in my room and study the map of the town and some of the other leaflets we were given by the tour company."

"I shall give my little monster another good scrub! Would you believe it, Janey, some idiot had painted over the original brass, which was why he looked so dirty. Possibly that is why he was undervalued, but by the time I have finished with him, he will look very handsome."

"I shall come and knock on your door about five o'clock," I suggested. "We could go down to the reception lounge and drink coffee and amuse ourselves watching our fellow guests, until Tim and Mike put in an appearance. How about it?"

Sally agreed, and when I went along to her room at the appointed time, she was waiting for me, looking lovelier than ever in a pale cream silk two-piece suit, with tiny emerald studs glowing on the lobes of her ears, and a fine chain gold necklet from which hung a single square-cut green stone, to relieve the plainness of her outfit.

I had decided to wear a long-sleeved, fine jersey dress of palest blue, with a shirred waist and a slit neckline. It was a dress I had worn at Christmas, when Mike had been at a party I had attended, and he had remarked then how much he liked it, but it hadn't been of Mike I had been thinking when I studied my reflection in the wardrobe mirror before leaving the bedroom.

Looking at myself in the glass, in my blue gown, with my straw-colored hair, wide-apart blue eyes, and tip-tilted nose, I did somewhat resemble the doll in the blue-and-white gingham dress which I had admired in the market that morning, as Dirk van der Woude had pointed out to me.

I had taken his remark as spurious flattery, certain that in my shapeless anorak, with my damp hair plastered against my blushing cheeks as he chatted me up beside his stall in the Lange Voorhout, I looked far from pretty, and I wished, wistfully, that he could see me as I looked now!

The afternoon sunshine had been of short du-

45

ration, and dark thunder clouds had swept back across the sky, bringing a steady downpour in their wake. As a consequence, when Sally and I went down to the lounge to wait for the arrival of Tim and Mike, we found it crowded with other guests, who had no desire to brave the storm and wander out on sightseeing tours.

We recognized several of the people who sat at the round, glass-topped tables as having traveled out on the same plane. The labels on their hand luggage indicated that they were on the same package holiday as we were, and a middle-aged couple, to whom we had spoken in the airport bus which had brought us from Schiphol to The Hague, waved to us to come and join them at their table, where there were two vacant chairs.

We chatted with them and drank coffee until Tim and Mike arrived at the hotel, looking extremely wet, but beaming with delight to see us.

"You look like a couple of half-drowned rats!" said Sally as we went over to greet them.

Mike made a mischievous grab to embrace her, but she skillfully avoided him, having no desire to have her pretty suit spoiled by contact with his damp coat.

"I think you should come up to the bedroom and dry yourselves," she suggested.

"I hope it doesn't rain like this on Saturday," grumbled Tim as he followed her to the lift. "Poor Anna is quite down in the dumps at the thought that it might. She is almost as superstitious as you are, Janey," he grinned at me, "and that's saying something!

"You know the kind of thing I'm talking about." He looked at Sally. "Happy the bride the sun shines on—which of course means bad luck if it rains, and then there is all the nonsense about having to wear something old, something new, something borrowed and something blue."

"I didn't think anyone could possibly be more superstitious than Janey!" Mike put in his oar, as he grinned across at me.

"Remember the time I brought you some red and white roses from the garden, to cheer you up after your bout of flu, and you nearly had a relapse and told me to take them away?"

His gaze strayed to Sally as he shook his head.

"I was heartbroken that day, thinking that my best girl was turning me down yet again, until she explained that it is unlucky to put red and white flowers together in a bunch, for some obscure reason which I have now forgotten.

"You wouldn't throw away a bouquet of roses if I gave them to you, would you?" he leered at my friend.

"You will not know the answer to that until you try it out!" she teased.

Mike laughed and into his eyes came the same gleam of interest with which Dirk van der Woude had regarded Sally earlier in the day.

"Here we go again," I thought, and I might have found the situation amusing if I had not been piqued at the knowledge that it was the men I liked best who so quickly deserted me for the pleasure of Sally's flirtatious banter.

We squeezed into the lift alongside another

group of guests, although everyone tried to steer clear of Mike and Tim in their wet coats.

"My room is very handy for the lift," said Sally when we got out at the second floor. "It's right here." She bent down to unlock her door. "Janey's is at the far end of the corridor."

Tim took off his coat and hung it over the bath so that the drips wouldn't wet the floor. He dried his hands and face and rubbed vigorously at his damp hair with the towel Sally handed to him. Mike did likewise.

"We were unlucky," Tim complained. "We couldn't get the car parked anywhere near the entrance to the Collenius. There wasn't a single space we could have squeezed into, and finally we had to go back to the car park in the square, a block away from here. That is why we got so wet," he bemoaned.

Mike crossed the room to look out of the window. Although it was only late afternoon, black storm clouds and the torrential rain made it seem dark as midnight outside.

"I don't think, even if it means that we shan't have the pleasure of initiating you into the mysteries of *Rijstafels* and *dagings* and *sambals* at Woo Ping's, we should venture out in this weather," he muttered with a shake of his head. "We would be soaked through before we got there."

"Woo Ping?" Sally echoed the name. "Surely that isn't what the place you were going to take us to is called?" she giggled. "It sounds most odd!"

48

"There is nothing odd about the food you get there!" retorted Mike. "To my way of thinking, it serves the best *Rijstafel* in town, as you will find out some other time." He smiled at Sally, and I felt the invitation that followed was for her alone. "You must let me take you there during your holiday."

Sally flushed faintly under his steady gaze, possibly remembering what I had told her in the afternoon about Mike having a soft spot for her, and she turned quickly to Tim, saying:

"If we aren't going to go to Woo Ping's, can you suggest somewhere nearer?"

"There is a Hungarian restaurant not far from here," I put in. "I was reading about it in our guidebook this afternoon, and they say it is worth a visit."

"De Zigeunerbaron is a good couple of hundred yards away from here." Mike shook his head. "We'd get soaked even going such a short distance. Just look at the rain!" He nodded towards the window. "It looks as if there had been a cloudburst."

"We don't need to go any further than the Collenius's own dining room for a good meal," said Tim. "Anna and I have had several meals here, and never been disappointed, which is saying something, since Anna is very fussy about what she eats."

"In that case, we shall grace the hotel dining room with our presence this evening!" said Sally gaily. "Thank goodness we don't have to venture outside," she went on with a shiver as a crackle of thunder overhead set the bottles of beauty preparations she had laid out on her dressing table dancing on the wooden surface. "I am a scaredy cat when it comes to thunderstorms."

Hurriedly she pulled the heavy curtain across the window to shut out the sight of the rain and the flickering lightning, and she jumped nervously as another deafening crash seemed to shake the building to its foundations.

Mike slipped a friendly arm around her waist and led her to the door.

"Come on, Sally. You need something to settle these nerves of yours, and I know the very thing. Come along, Tim. Let's find out if the girls know the correct way to drink *bessengenever!*"

## Chapter 4

Tim led the way to the little cocktail bar which was tucked into a corner at the back of the main lounge of the Collenius.

The storm had kept most of the hotel guests indoors and both the lounge and the bar were packed with disgruntled tourists. Mike insinuated his way past the tables and the groups of young people who were standing near the high, wood-paneled bar counter, and miraculously managed to find a couple of vacant stools for Sally and me to sit on.

With a wink at Tim, he ordered four *bessengenevers*, which turned out to be black currant gin. When we lifted our glasses to take our first taste of this unusual drink, he told us, with a mischievous grin, that we must not sip from the glass, but follow the local custom and gulp down the liquid, whereupon he proceeded to show us how it should be done.

After my first attempt, which brought stinging tears to my eyes as the gin ran over the back of my throat, I decided, with Sally, that local customs could go by the board as far as we were concerned, and thereafter we took slow, cautious sips of the *genever*, between long bouts of conversation.

When Tim had telephoned in the afternoon to say that his fiancée would not be able to come to The Hague with him that evening to be introduced to me, I had been very disappointed. I had been looking forward to meeting Anna, but as the evening progressed, I was quite glad that she had had to opt out of the dinner party arrangements.

Had she come, there was no doubt that Tim would have concentrated his attention on her, and since Mike was oblivious to everyone but Sally, I would have been very much the odd woman out.

As it was, however, Tim was eager to hear the latest news from home—the kind of chitchat that is so difficult to convey in a letter, so the pair of us talked away ten to the dozen about what was happening on the family farm in Angus and about what our friends in the neighborhood were doing. Most important, as far as Tim was concerned, I was able to tell him about the improvements that were being made to the smaller of the two farmhouses on the estate— the one which was to be home for his Dutch wife and himself.

I also told him about the reception being planned for the pair of them at Garthland when they arrived back from the honeymoon. I mentioned that I was not sure if I would manage to get time off from the hospital to attend this function, but I would do my best to wangle it.

Our parents had been very disappointed at not being able to attend Tim's wedding in Holland, but our mother suffers from a form of claustrophobia, which makes it an ordeal for her to stay for any length of time in an enclosed space. This rules out any lengthy journeys in trains and buses, and travel by air is quite out of the question as far as she is concerned.

She had once forced herself to fly to Italy on holiday, since Father was keen to revisit some of the places he had known as a soldier when he had fought there in World War II, but the result of this flight had been a near-nervous breakdown, so that had put paid to the idea of flying as a means of getting to the Continent on holiday.

Father did not want to come to Holland without her, and our sister was expecting her third child at the end of the month, which meant that I was the only member of the family who could possibly make it to the wedding in Anna's hometown. Tim was extremely grateful to me, and to Sally, for coming to support him on his big day.

"Anna was so upset that she couldn't manage to come and meet you before Saturday," sighed my brother. "However, I have talked so much about you, she says you won't seem a complete stranger when you eventually meet!

"I am quite sure you will like Anna," he went on happily. "In some ways she reminds me of you. Possibly it is the way you both tease me," he grinned.

I smiled back at him, happy to see him look so happy.

"You know," he went on, "Anna was very touched when I told her you were trying to learn Dutch for her sake. How is it going, by the way?"

"Not badly at all." Sally switched her attention from Mike to reply for me. "I wish I could pick up a foreign language as quickly as Janey can. She is wasted as a children's nurse. Considering all the qualifications she has—typing, shorthand, French, German and I don't know what all—she should be aiming for one of the top jobs in the European Secretariat!"

"I'm not high-powered enough for that kind of post," I said, aware of my own limitations. "And in any case, I like working with children."

Mike ordered another two *genevers* for Tim and himself, and while he waited for the barman to bring them, I glanced at my watch.

"What time do you think we should eat?" I asked.

"I thought about eight thirty," said Tim.

"Isn't that rather late?" I frowned.

"Hungry as usual, Janey?" grinned Mike. "I have never known anyone else with your capacity for tucking into a hearty meal, without adding a millimeter to your waistline!"

"It wasn't me, it was you I was thinking about!" I retorted. "You surely haven't forgotten that you have a long drive back to Bolsward tonight, and it won't be a very pleasant one in the dark, in this storm."

"There is nothing for you to worry about, Janey," grinned Tim reassuringly. "I forgot to mention to you that Mike and I are staying the night in The Hague."

"That's right," Mike nodded. "I have arranged to spend a week or so with a friend here, before returning to England. I originally intended to go home after Tim's wedding, but when he told me that you and Sally were going to spend a holiday here, I decided to stay on. I thought," he continued amiably, "that you might like to have a handsome young man-about-town on hand to act as your escort while you were in The Hague." His eyes strayed to Sally. "After all, it isn't every day I get the chance of entertaining two of my favorite girls!"

I laughed.

"I can see you have learned other things besides looking after Fresian cattle and running a dairy farm at the College in Bolsward where you have been working!" I chaffed him. "This is the first flattering remark you have ever made to me."

"You would never let me pay you a compliment," he grinned, turning to Sally once again and saying:

"Do you know that for years I tried to ask Janey to be my special girl, and she just laughed at me! She very nearly gave me a complex about women. I thought I must be unattractive to them. What do you think?" he challenged her, eyes twinkling.

"I think Janey showed more sense than I would have credited her with," she replied blithely.

"Now you are at it!" He uttered a mock groan. "Undermining my self-confidence! It isn't good for me!"

"Nothing could undermine your self-confidence, Mike Russell." I pooh-poohed the idea. "Don't forget, I have known you most of your life, and I know what I am talking about."

"I don't know why I continue to like you, Janey Mathieson," he retorted mournfully. "You never take me seriously. I shall just have to drown my sorrows."

He raised his glass dramatically and gulped down his *genever* with such a lugubrious expression on his face that Sally and I couldn't help laughing at him.

Tim finished his own drink and suggested that after all it might be a good idea to dine early. In view of the continuing rainstorm, many of the hotel guests who might otherwise have gone elsewhere for their evening meal, as we ourselves had originally intended to do, might now decide to dine in the hotel's famous Vermeer Room.

We inched our way from the cocktail bar through the lounge toward the broad corridor which led to the dining room.

Mike and Sally walked ahead, with Tim and I following. We were separated from them momentarily as a boisterous crowd of young folk shoved past us, and we had to stand for almost a minute between two tables on the perimeter of the open plan lounge, before we could reach the corridor.

As we stood there, waiting to move on, once again I had the sensation that someone was watching me.

I glanced covertly down at the tables beside which we were standing. A group of youngsters was seated at one, all bar one of them laughing and talking at the top of their voices. The silent one was slumped in his seat, a scowl on his face, as if he resented the noisy talk around him. He was wearing a blue polo-neck cotton shirt, over which his greasy dark hair trailed untidily. I could not make out if it was he who was watching me, because he was wearing very dark-lensed sunglasses set in butterfly-shaped frames, which somehow emphasized the sickly pallor of his skin and the sullen pout of his lips.

At the other table, a middle-aged couple and a man in his early fifties, or so I judged by his graying hair, were seated. The solitary man's eyes slanted quickly away from me when I glanced casually in his direction, and he bent forward, so that I had no time to catch more than a glimpse of his features as he leaned across the table to tip the ash from the expensive cigar he was smoking into the glass ashtray on the far side.

His sudden movement distracted my attention from his face to his hand, which was badly scarred and puckered, as though it had been burned at some time. The fingers were stubby and callused and the nails dirt-ingrained, not at all like the fingers of the type of man I would associate with expensive cigars and places like the Collenius.

Tim distracted my attention from my discreet study of the strangers by nudging me forward again. We somehow managed to elbow our way through the groups of noisy teenagers who were struggling to get to the bar, and made our way up the broad, short flight of stairs which led to the entre-sol where the Vermeer Room was located.

The dining room was long and high-ceilinged, and although massive glass chandeliers hung from the ceiling, the faceted crystal merely reflected the flickering lights from the scarlet candles on the tables below.

The walls were wood-paneled, and the central one was decorated with a single, beautiful painting, which I took to be a genuine Vermeer. Ruby-red velvet curtains covered the full expanse of the window side of the room, and the rich material gleamed lustrously in the soft, dimly romantic light.

In spite of the size of the room, the tasteful decoration and the discreet lighting gave it an atmosphere of intimacy, and the tables were placed far enough apart so that conversation could not be overheard from one to the other.

I surmised that the price of the meals here would be in keeping with the luxury of the surroundings, and it was no doubt for this reason that Tim and Mike deliberately refused to let

Sally or me study the ornate menu cards, telling us that there was no need for us to look at them, since they intended to chose a truly Dutch meal for us.

The first course, a herring cocktail served in a balloon-shaped glass and garnished with lemon and chopped parsley, was superb. In turn, we each tried to guess what the "something" was that had been added to the mayonnaise to give it its unusual flavor, but none of us agreed on the ingredient. In the end we had to ask the waiter, who confirmed that it was a dash of port, as Tim had guessed, which gave the sauce its special piquancy.

"Anna is a wonderful cook," my brother enthused about his bride-to-be. "I expect that is how I managed to guess right. She will be able to give you a number of interesting Dutch recipes when you come to visit us."

"I wouldn't mind being told this particular recipe," said Sally, as she relished the last mouthful of her herring cocktail.

While she and my brother discussed various local dishes, Mike told me something about the work he had been doing at the Dutch College.

We spent some time over the meal. Course succeeded course, each one more unusual and appetizing than the previous one. When we had eaten the last of the succulent fresh strawberries which we had all chosen for dessert, Tim asked me if I had any recent snapshots from home, as he would like to have some to show Anna.

"Yes, I do." I smiled. "Right here."

I bent down to pick up my handbag from under the table, and Mike made a humorous remark about its size and asked me if I always carried a hold-all around with me.

"You men are lucky," I pointed out. "You have pockets in which to stow things, which we women don't have. As for the size of my bag, when I am on holiday I like to have one which is big enough to carry personal documents and things like tickets and passport, and my small bits and pieces of jewelry which I don't like leaving in the hotel bedroom.

"One never knows who has access to one's room, what with different chambermaids going in at night to turn down the beds, and housekeepers supervising that they have done their work properly."

"You do have a suspicious mind, don't you?" grinned Tim.

"That comes from years of living in hotels and the like," I shrugged, as I pulled out a bundle of envelopes held together with a broad rubber band, and flicked through them. To my annoyance, the photographs were not among them.

"I remember now," I muttered in a disgruntled tone. "I took the snaps out of my bag when we came back to the hotel this afternoon and put them in my suitcase, along with the guidebooks and brochures, so that they wouldn't get crumpled."

I pushed back my chair. "I shall run up to my room and get them, while you order coffee and liqueurs."

"Don't bother, Janey," Tim demurred.

"It's no trouble at all," I assured him. "In any case, I want to show them to Mike. I am sure he will appreciate my photography!"

I hurried upstairs and along the corridor to my room. The lock was stiff, and the key required a couple of turns to open the door.

A draft of air blasted against me as I entered, and in the light from the hall I could see the curtain that covered the french window which opened on to a ledgelike balcony, billow out wildly in the gusting wind and rain.

Without waiting to switch on the light, I dashed across to the window and slammed it shut. The locking device appeared to be loose, because another gust of wind almost forced it open again, so I got hold of the chair which was beside the writing desk and wedged its wooden back under the handle to secure the catch. As a further precaution, since I wanted to be sure that even the strongest gust would not be able to force the window open again and allow rain to come flooding into the room, I maneuvered the heavy desk against the chair, and breathing deeply after my efforts at furniture shifting, I recrossed the room to shut the door and switch on the light.

In its bright glare I noticed that the bed cover had been turned down by the chambermaid, and my nightgown placed neatly on top of the pillow. In the bathroom cubicle, fresh towels had replaced the ones I had used earlier in the evening.

I approved of these services, but I did not approve of the way my pretty doll had been removed from the pillow, where I had laid her, and flung higgledy-piggledy on to the floor, and I most certainly did not approve of the fact that the maid had been tampering with my personal possessions.

Living in hostels and bed-sitters as I had done for the past three years, I had learned the value of tidiness. When you eat, sleep and entertain in a single room, it has to be kept immaculate in order not to seem dingy and unattractive, and I have got into the habit of arranging my things in a neat and orderly manner. As a result of this, one glance at the dressing table quickly indicated that someone had been playing around with my makeup box; even the carton of paper tissues was ruffled.

Frowning, I opened the drawers where I had carefully laid my underclothes, and I experienced a sense of outrage when I found that they too had been moved around. The dresses which I had hung in the wardrobe had not missed the attention of the nosey maid. They drooped askew from their hangers, and my shoes had been scattered over the cupboard floor.

Hot with indignation, I hurriedly put things to rights, retrieved the photographs from my suitcase, which, oddly enough, had not been tampered with, and hurried back to the dining room to rejoin my friends.

I did not say anything to them about the chambermaid's impertinence, although I determined to tackle the floor manager about the matter in the morning.

However, I soon forgot my annoyance as I showed off my photographs to Tim and Mike, who chuckled with amusement at some of the ones I myself had taken. In my usual manner, I had somehow managed to behead or to remove the feet of the people I was snapping, and the results of some of my attempts were hilarious.

The evening flew past so quickly that it was only when Tim noticed that we were the only guests left in the Vermeer Room and the staff was discreetly setting the tables for breakfast, that we realized that it was past midnight.

"Thank goodness we don't have to drive back to Bolsward tonight!" Tim stifled a yawn as he signaled the waiter to bring the bill. "I think I would have fallen asleep at the wheel. All that talking and laughing and eating have made me very sleepy."

"To say nothing of all the schnapps you and Mike have been imbibing!" put in Sally.

Mike leered at her.

"I was merely trying to get a little Dutch courage in order to ask you if you could put up with my company tomorrow? Tim will be leaving for Bolsward at crack of dawn, and I shall be all alone in a strange town."

He eyed her soulfully as he added:

"You will let me come with you wherever you are going, won't you?"

"That depends," she replied airily. "We have already made our arrangements for tomorrow.

We intend to set off early to go to Keukenhof to see the flowers, and you don't look to me like the kind of man who would enjoy spending hours strolling around looking at tulips."

"It would depend who I was with," he grinned at her. "But as it happens, I am very fond of flowers. Ones like these are among my favorites!"

He carefully extracted an amethyst-colored anemone from the vase on the table, and presented it to Sally with a flourish.

"Wear that when I call at the hotel for you at nine o'clock, and I'll know you love me!" His eyes flirted with her.

Sally tucked the flower into the V line of her suit and Mike smiled and slipped an arm around her waist as we followed Tim from the room. The sideways glance I shot at my friend told me that she was thoroughly enjoying Mike's flirtatious manner, and I was sure she would not object to his company on our excursion to Keukenhof.

"I shall see you on Saturday." Tim gave me a brotherly hug as we came to the hotel exit. "And Janey," there was a nervous tremor in his voice as he added, "I am so glad one of my family will be present to support me on my wedding day!"

Sally and I stood in the shelter of the porch watching Mike and Tim as they made their way along the dark, narrow, rain-swept street, until they turned to wave a final good night to us when they reached the corner of the block.

"I enjoyed tonight immensely, didn't you?" Sally took my arm companionably as we retreated into the warmth of the hotel. "Mike is good fun, isn't he? He isn't as shy as he used to be," she chuckled. "I'm glad we shall be seeing more of him while we are in The Hague."

"Poor Tim!" I yawned sleepily. "Toward the end of the evening, I could see he was beginning to feel a trifle nervous about his wedding."

I shook my head. "It must be quite a thought, deciding that you want to give up a sort of freedom, to live with one person for the rest of your life."

"A pleasant thought, I would imagine, if it is the right person you give it up for," remarked Sally. "From the way Tim talks about his Anna, I think he has found the right person for him."

We went over to the lift and pressed the button to take us to our floor. When we got out, I noticed a movement at the far end of the corridor outside my room, and for a second I thought that the man I saw there had been at my door, but a second glance confirmed that he was at the one next to it, and having the same difficulty I had had earlier in getting his key to turn in the lock.

"It really has been a lovely day," Sally sighed contentedly as she took her room key from her bag.

"If I'm not down in the breakfast room by eight thirty," I murmured as she fitted it into the lock, "come to my room and keep knocking on the door until you wake me up." I stifled another yawn. "As you say, it has been quite a day, and I am so tired I could sleep the clock around!"

Sally smiled. "If the rest of our holiday is going to be on a par with today," she remarked as she pushed the door open, "we shall need another one to give us time to recover and be fit for work again!"

I laughed. "That's exactly how I feel at the moment. Good night, Sally, and sleep well."

"I certainly shall," she sighed happily. "See you in the morning."

I strolled along the passage to my room, wondering, as I passed the man who was still having difficulty trying to unlock his door, if I should offer to help, but almost immediately decided against this, for there was something about his fumbling movements which made me think he had perhaps been drinking too much.

His back was toward me, and I hurried past him to my own door, which on this occasion I was able to unlock without difficulty. This was just as well, for the man made an unexpected movement toward me. Hastily I slipped into my room, slamming the door behind me and making sure that not only did I turn the key in the lock, but also that the extra bolt above the handle was pushed into position. I had no desire to tangle with a drunken Romeo who seemed to want my company!

Although the wind was still buffeting the window, the barrier I had set up when I returned to the room for the photographs would have kept even the wildest of tornadoes from forcing it open, and in spite of my moment of nervousness when the stranger had lunged at me I now felt safe and secure in my comfortable room, and wasted no time in getting into bed.

I was too tired, after a surfeit of rich food, cheerful conversation and the fine liqueur brandy I had taken with the after-dinner coffee, to take a bath, and I even found it an effort to remove my makeup, before giving myself a cat-lick and crawling between the sheets.

Soon I drifted into blissful unconsciousness, too tired to notice the forks of lightning which penetrated through the thick fabric of the curtains; too tired to hear the rattling of the window as if some demented creature of the storm was trying to force an entry; too tired to be disturbed by the crashing of the thunder overhead; too tired even to dream.

It was not until I woke up, shortly after seven o'clock, that I hazily recalled all the events of the previous day. I turned over, closed my eyes and went to sleep again, wondering, as I dozed off, if I would have the pleasure of a further meeting with Dirk van der Woude.

## Chapter 5

There was a noise in my ears like the buzzing of a swarm of bees. I forced my eyelids open, and as sleep receded, I realized that what I was hearing was the insistent call of the phone by my bedside.

Feeling faintly annoyed because I had been roused from a pleasant reverie in which Dirk van der Woude figured, I stretched out my arm to lift up the receiver.

Who on earth could be calling me at this hour of the morning, I wondered as I muttered my name into the microphone.

It was Sally.

"Janey, I feel awful!" she moaned. "I think it was something I ate last night. In fact," she sniffed, "I know it was! I should have resisted those gorgeous strawberries. I've been allergic to them since childhood—but they looked so tempting!"

"I'll get dressed and come to your room right away."

"No! No! There's no need for that!" she protested. "I can take care of myself. I always carry
pills for what I call Spanish, French, or Italian
tummy, depending on where I am—Dutch
tummy in this instance, and I shall be all right if
I eat nothing for a few hours and drink lots of
liquid."

"You're sure?"

"Quite sure, Janey. What I was calling you for
was to ask if you have Mike's phone number, so
that you could tell him that we shan't be going
to Keukenhof today." She sighed with a disappointment.

I shook my head.

I'm afraid I don't have his address in The
Hague, but I shall explain what has happened
when he comes along to the hotel. I'm sure he
will understand."

"I feel mean, letting you down like this, when
we had planned to spend the day at Keukenhof,
especially now that the sun is actually shining at
last."

At her words I glanced across at the window.
I hadn't as yet pulled back the curtains, but
through the woven fabric I could see a golden
gleam. There was no sound of the gale-force
wind which had raged during the night, and I
felt relieved, for often a violent storm presages a
spell of good weather, and if this was the case,
Anna would be a very happy bride tomorrow,
with the sun shining on her.

"Don't worry about me, Sally. We can go to
Keukenhof another day. The tulips will still be

blooming on Monday," I assured her. "You take your medicine and stay in bed for the morning. I shall be along to see you in about ten minutes. In fact," I went on, "I shall telephone room service to bring a pot of tea for two to your room, and I shall have a cup with you before I go down for breakfast."

"Janey, that is kind of you, but I do feel I am upsetting your day."

"Don't be silly!" I yawned. "I shall enjoy having a wander around the town on my own. See you in a little while."

I replaced the receiver and after a slow, lazy stretch, I got out of bed.

Poor Sally! It was hard luck that she should be off-color at the outset of her holiday, and more especially on the very day that Mike Russell had planned to spend with us. I sensed that it was Mike, rather than me, she was upset about letting down.

I telephoned the floor waiter and asked him to take tea for two along to Sally's room in a quarter of an hour. Then I crossed the floor, heaved aside the chair and the desk with which I had barricaded the window against the gusting wind the night before, and pulled aside the curtains to let the sunlight come flooding into the room.

Early though it was, I could feel the heat of the sun on my body as I stood by the window in my gossamer-thin nightdress, and I smiled contentedly as I stared out at the cloudless blue sky.

There wasn't even the whisper of a breeze to

stir the young green leaves of the plane trees whose tops I could glimpse from where I was standing, and I was convinced that my earlier deduction was correct, and that we were in for a spell of sunny weather.

It was going to be a superb day, and just for a brief second I regretted that we wouldn't be able to go to Keukenhof today. However, I had been told that there were several lovely parks in The Hague, so I could visit them on my own if I got tired of wandering around the town.

I opened the french window and stepped out on to the narrow balcony, to take a deep breath of the fresh, warm air, which was sweetly scented with the perfume of the lilacs in the garden below.

As I leaned over the railing to admire the deep purple plumes of the flowers, I noticed that a crowd of people was gathered at the foot of the fire escape steps which led past the outside wall of my bedroom. At my movement, several of the men glanced upward, and I hastily withdrew from the balcony, hoping that no one had seen me.

I crossed the room and entered the bath cubicle to turn on the taps, and while I waited for the bath to fill up I laid out the clothes I was going to wear.

I scattered a handful of pine-scented salts into the water, stepped into the bath, and had just immersed myself when the telephone rang.

I let it ring for a few moments before, with a grimace of annoyance, I stepped from the water, wrapped myself in a bath towel, and went to answer the summons.

To my surprise, it was the manager of the hotel who was calling.

"Did you sleep well last night, Miss Mathieson?" he inquired.

Somewhat taken aback by the question, I paused before replying.

"Yes. Yes. I slept very well," I said at last.

"Nothing disturbed you?"

"Disturbed me?" I echoed. "Oh! You mean the storm," I replied, feeling somewhat overwhelmed at the unusual interest the management of the Collenius took in the comfort of its guests. "Yes, it was a bit disconcerting, and I was afraid the wind was going to force open the french window, because of the loose catch. However, I wedged a chair under the handle and that did the trick. I slept like a log!"

"You didn't hear any unusual noises?" It was a different voice which asked this question.

"I only heard the rattling of the wind," I repeated, pulling the bath towel tightly around me to absorb trickles of water which were running down my spine. "As I have said, I slept like a log, until a short time ago. Now, if you don't mind, I shall hang up." I shivered as more icy drops chilled my skin. "I was having a bath when you rang, and I am still dripping wet!"

"I am so sorry to have inconvenienced you, madam," said the suave voice. "Good morning."

What a very odd call, I thought as I replaced the receiver and briskly toweled myself dry. If the manager went through this rigamarole with all of his guests, it must take up a lot of his time!

I pulled on a pair of rust-colored slacks, tucked the tail of a rust-colored silk shirt beneath the waistband, slipped on a pair of canvas sandals, and making sure that I had everything I required in my bag, I went along to see Sally.

At my knock she opened the door and gave me a wan smile.

"Trust me to do something silly!" she pouted. "When I see what a glorious day it is, I feel furious with myself for letting those strawberries tempt me last night!"

She retired to her bed and pulled the covers over her, so that only her pale face, the dark circles under her eyes emphasizing the pallor, was visible.

"You poor soul!" I murmured sympathetically. "You do look washed out!"

I was about to close the bedroom door when the waiter appeared with the tea I had ordered. I took the tray from him and carried it to the bedside table.

"Trust me to be sick today of all days!" groaned Sally, staring toward the window through which the sunlight streamed. "It wouldn't have been so bad if it had been yesterday, when it was so wet, and when we hadn't a date with Mike."

"You would have missed getting your dragon, in that case." I tried to console her, picking up

73

the ornament which was lying on her dressing table, and looking at it with less distaste than I had when I had bought it at the market.

"You know, now that you've polished it up a bit, it doesn't look quite so mean and menacing! I might even grow to like him!" I smiled, trying to cheer her up.

"He's all right," Sally replied listlessly, the reason for her apathy quickly apparent as she added, "You will explain to Mike that I'm not well, won't you? I don't want him to think that I am making an excuse not to go out with him."

"No one stays in bed on a lovely, sunny holiday morning, unless they have to!" I laughed. "Of course Mike will know you wouldn't make up a story like that to avoid him!"

I poured out the tea and drank a cup with her. When she had finished her drink I tucked her comfortably beneath the covers, reassured her that Mike wouldn't be upset about the change of plan, and went down to the breakfast room.

There was a lot of coming and going in the reception hall when I stepped from the lift, with people standing about in groups and chatting excitedly, and I spotted a number of uniformed police in the hall.

I wondered curiously what was happening as I made my way toward the dining room, but the murmured conversations I could overhear were not enlightening.

"Janey!"

I heard my name called out, and turned to

look back along the broad corridor. Mike, his usual broad grin on his face, waved a hand to attract my attention as he came striding toward me. Almost at the same time, a man detached himself from the cluster of people who were standing near the reception desk, and my heart stupidly seemed to miss a beat as I recognized Dirk van der Woude.

He stared across at me, and I was about to smile at him, when Mike stepped up to me, blocking van der Woude from my line of vision as he slipped his arm around my waist and gave me an affectionate kiss on the cheek.

"Good morning, Janey, my love!" he greeted me. "How is my best girl this morning? Wasn't it good of me to lay on the sunshine for our trip to Keukenhof?" He smiled as he urged me toward the door of the breakfast room.

"Mike!" I exclaimed. "You are far too early. I haven't had breakfast yet."

"Neither have I," he replied. "I thought I would add to the pleasure of the day by taking it with you and Sally. Where is she, by the way?"

"She is still in bed, I'm sorry to say," I told him, trying to peer over his shoulder to see if van der Woude was still there.

"Don't tell me she has slept in," grinned Mike. "I thought she would have got up with the lark, for the pleasure of my company!"

"I'm sure she would have," I sighed, "but unfortunately, she's eaten something to which she is allergic, and that has put paid to our plans to visit Keukenhof today."

Mike's face fell.

"What bad luck! Is there anything we can do for her?"

"A day's fast, perhaps merely a morning's fast, and she should be right as rain. She will need to be," I went on. "We can't have her missing tomorrow's wedding."

"Good heavens, no!" exclaimed Mike. "We certainly can't have that! Tim and I are counting on you two to hold our end up with the Dutch party."

A long table was set out in the middle of the breakfast room, with plates piled with various types of bread and rolls, and platters of cold sliced meats and sausages and cheese.

We helped ourselves to what we wanted, adding neat containers of jams and butters to our load as we went to sit at a table near the window.

Mike tried to signal a waiter to bring coffee, but the man was too preoccupied with whatever he was discussing with a fellow waiter, to notice us.

"The hotel seems to be buzzing with excitement this morning," I remarked to Mike. "Even the staff seem worked up about something. I wonder what is going on?"

"I noticed a police car in the street, and yes, I did notice a couple of officers in the hall when I came in," observed Mike. "I expect it's because the Mambalukes are staying here. They invariably seem to create a disturbance wherever they are appearing. That is why there were so many teenagers besieging the cocktail bar and lounge last night. They were wanting a close up of their idols."

He shook his head. "You know, it's a funny thing. The queen, or any member of the royal family, or a world-famous musician or actor can walk down the street here, without anyone giving them a second glance, but let one of the way-out, off-beat pop groups appear, and the youngsters go almost berserk! That is why the police will be in evidence here today—to stop any trouble before it starts."

"Ah!" I nodded my head. "That also explains the rather unusual call I had from the hotel manager this morning." I told Mike how I had been asked if I had had a disturbed night, adding, "I didn't even hear the thunder, far less the noisy screams of the pop group fans. The minute my head hit the pillow, I was fast asleep!"

We finished breakfast and made our way out into Molen Straat. As we strolled through the reception hall, I caught another glimpse of van der Woude, and I couldn't help wondering what had brought him to the Collenius. He gave me a brief smile, which somehow lacked the friendliness of his manner of yesterday, and then turned to talk to his companions.

Mike and I spent a very pleasant morning wandering around the city center, admiring the historic buildings and the long, straight canal which reflected the flowering chestnut trees lining it.

I was amused, when we were walking through

the exclusive Lange Poten shopping precinct, to come across a restaurant called Sir Edward, and a little further on, another restaurant called The Angus Steakhouse. In fact, the number of foreign names and signs I came across gave The Hague an extremely cosmopolitan flavor.

We bought ice creams from a gaily decorated cart at the corner of the street, and ate them on a seat which overlooked the charming lake of Hofvijver. Its small island and the fountain spraying water high into the air formed a scintillating screen between us and our view of the handsome Gothic and Renaissance buildings of the Binnenhof.

We chatted spasmodically of old times and future plans, but mainly of Sally. It amused me how often our conversation seemed to come back to my friend, and I came to the conclusion that I had been nearer the mark than I had imagined, when I had teased Sally the previous afternoon by saying that it was she and not I who attracted the attention of my brother's friend.

"Janey, do you think that Sally would find living in the country dull after the years she has spent in the city?"

Mike tried to make the query sound off-hand, but by this time I was growing impatient with his incessant questioning. I wasn't jealous of my friend, but I did think that when Mike was with me, he might at least make a pretense of being interested in me and my affairs.

"Why don't you ask her yourself?" I remarked brusquely. "It is past mid-day, and it is quite possible that Sally is feeling better and would like someone to talk to. She might even be up and about, and happy to join us for a light lunch."

"That's an idea!" Mike seized on my suggestion with alacrity. "She might even feel well enough to go to Scheveningen this afternoon." His enthusiasm grew. "We could go for a walk along the sands. The sea breeze would be good for her."

He strode along the street toward the hotel at such a vigorous pace that I found difficulty in keeping up with him, and by the time we arrived at the Collenius I was out of breath.

"Look! There's Sally over there!" A wide beam spread over Mike's face when we walked into the reception hall.

He hurried ahead of me to the table where Sally was seated, chatting to a group of people among whom I recognized Natasha Berg and Saunders, the TV actor, and also, to my surprise and secret pleasure, Dirk van der Woude.

"Hi, Sally!" Mike greeted her from halfway across the room.

Sally looked around in surprise.

"Hello, you two! I wasn't expecting you back until evening!" She gave a shake of her head. "I told Janey she was not to worry about me."

"It was Mike who was doing the worrying," I remarked dryly, though I doubt if either of them heard me.

"How are you feeling now?" Mike was looking

anxiously down at Sally, ignoring the looks of her friends as they stared up at him.

"Slightly fragile!" Sally smiled at him in reply. "But not fragile enough to stay in my room with all the excitement that was going on in the corridor and in the garden below the window. I couldn't have fallen asleep again, even if I had wanted to, and in any case, my curiosity got the better of me and I simply had to find out what was going on!"

Mike and Sally continued to look at each other as if there was no one else present, and I felt embarrassed and awkward at the way they were ignoring me, so that my voice sounded sharp even to my own ears as I said brusquely:

"Mike told me that there was a well-known pop group staying in the hotel overnight, which would explain why the bar was invaded by teen-agers yesterday evening, and no doubt why the police were in evidence here this morning."

Sally managed to drag her attention from Mike, and look at me.

"Janey, it wasn't because of the pop group that the police came to the Collenius. I'll explain what the fuss was about in a moment, but first," she turned to Mike once again, "I shall have to introduce Mike to my friends.

"This is Natasha Berg, Mike Russell and Janey Mathieson," she introduced us to each of the members of her party, finally saying, "and this is Dirk van der Woude, Mike. Remember I told you about him last night—how he came to

80

the rescue of Janey and me when we were attacked by the bag snatcher."

Dirk and Mike acknowledged the introduction, each considering the other with a certain reserve, as if they were both aware of the other's interest in my attractive friend and were weighing their chances with her.

For the first time in my life, I was jealous of Sally. It wasn't fair, I thought bitterly, that she should prove so attractive to the two men I liked, that neither of them spared me a second glance, for Mike kept his gaze focused on Sally, while Dirk's blue eyes watched the pair of them with frowning intensity.

Once again I tried to break the spell Sally cast over them.

"You haven't yet told Mike and me what the fuss was about," I reminded her, as Dirk pulled out a chair for me.

"A young man was found dead at the foot of one of the hotel fire escapes," she informed us. "The one at the end of the corridor beside your bedroom, Janey. The police can't decide if he fell down while trying to get into the hotel to see some girl—the iron rungs of the ladder were very slippery with the overnight rain, and he could have missed his footing. On the other hand, they think he could have been high on LSD, and simply walked out of one of the windows which led on to the fire escape, and fallen over the guard rail."

I shuddered. "How horrible! Do they know who he was?"

Sally shook her head.

"According to the hotel manager, he was not a guest here, but then they might not want to admit to it," she shrugged. "It would be bad publicity."

"The barman remembers serving him a drink early on in the evening," put in Saunders, "but he doesn't remember seeing him after that, but that isn't to be wondered at considering how crowded with youngsters his bar became later on."

"No one else remembers seeing him," shrugged Natasha, "but again that isn't surprising. All the young people look pretty much alike these days, with their untidy hair, the jeans and their T shirts."

"This particular youth wasn't wearing a T shirt," put in van der Woude. "He was dressed in jeans and a blue polo-neck cotton pullover."

I looked up with a start, remembering that I had noticed a young man similarly dressed, seated at the table in the lounge beside which Tim and I had stopped when we had been separated from Sally and Mike by the horde of teenagers.

"He didn't happen to be wearing dark glasses?" I asked.

Everyone at the table turned to look at me, and Sally exclaimed.

"I heard someone say something about a pair of sunglasses being found broken near the body! Why did you ask?"

"I noticed a young man with a blue polo-neck

shirt in the lounge when we were going to the Vermeer Room, but," I shrugged, "I expect there are as many youths with blue polo necks and dark glasses as there are ones with black jackets and balaclavas."

"Could you describe what your one looked like?" asked Mike.

"Darkish hair, pale face. There was nothing very striking about his features. His fancy, butterfly-shaped glasses were the most noticeable thing about him."

Saunders was staring at me as if he was actually noticing me for the first time, and automatically assuming the part of the TV detective he plays, he said in an authoritative voice:

"I think you should have a word with the officer in charge about this. It might be of some help to them."

I wished I had held my tongue about the glasses, and I tried to wriggle out of the situation by saying, "I'm sure I would only be wasting police time if I did so." I shook my head. "I very much doubt if the young man I saw is the same one they are trying to trace. In fact," I added more firmly, "I am quite sure he isn't. My young man was in the company of a group of other young people, and surely, if they were friendly with him, they would have come forward to say if he was missing?"

"Of course they would," agreed Natasha, who had been left out of the limelight for too long and now wanted to have her say. "And I don't think the police would be very pleased if you went to them with useless information. They will have had plenty of that already."

Sally, Mike and the others nodded in agreement, but from the expression on Dirk van der Woude's face, I gathered that he was not in accord with Natasha's advice.

Since I wanted to appear in a favorable light as far as he was concerned, instead of agreeing with her, as I had been on the point of doing, I said slowly, "I shall compromise. I don't want to get involved in something which might upset my plans for tomorrow's wedding, but when I come back to The Hague after the celebrations are over, if there have been no developments, and if the lad has still not been identified, I shall go to them with my story."

## Chapter 6

Oliver Saunders, having been made aware of my
existence, for some reason now seemed determined to maintain an interest in me.

"What wedding are you talking about?" he
leered at me. "Not your own, I hope?"

I shook my head. "No. No. My brother is marrying a Dutch girl tomorrow, in a little village
near Bolsward."

"Bolsward?" he repeated. "In Friesland? Why,
I've been there! We filmed a thriller in the
neighborhood a couple of years ago, do you
remember, Bob?" He glanced across the table
at a thin young man who was seated beside
Natasha, and whom I had been told was their
director. "We could hardly move for cows," he
grinned. "There seemed to be more of them
about than people!"

"Cows?" Natasha grimaced. "I'm glad I
wasn't with you then. I can't stand the crea-
tures!"

"Yes, it was as well you weren't in that partic-

85

ular film," shrugged Saunders, and the expression in his eyes as they rested for a brief second on Natasha indicated that he didn't much care for his leading lady. "You might have found yourself playing second fiddle to a bovine beauty! They practically worship cows in Friesland! Holland isn't all tulips, any more than Amsterdam is all art galleries or drugs and diamonds, you know!" he informed her in a scathing voice.

Natasha ignored his remarks and addressed Sally.

"Are you going to this wedding as well?"

Sally nodded. "Yes, I am. And Mike there," her smiling gaze rested on the man facing her, "is to be best man. We are all looking forward to it. I haven't been to a wedding in a foreign country before."

"And if you are going to attend this one, my love," Mike smiled back at her, "let me remind you that you will have to get up at the crack of dawn, to give yourself plenty of time to put on your glad rags, and be ready waiting for me at the entrance at the hotel when I call for you at seven thirty!"

"I didn't realize we would be leaving so early!" gasped Sally. "It's not fair," she pouted. "I like to have a long lie when I am on holiday."

"It is a three-hour drive to Anna's home," Mike reminded her, "so we can't afford to leave any later. The civil ceremony is at ten thirty, and I have to be by Mike's side before then.

"However, driving in the early morning has its

benefits," he consoled her. "There won't be much traffic about, and we should make good time, apart from having a chance to admire the scenery en route, which is very lovely, especially if the sun is shining."

"So you aren't just here for your brother's wedding?" Saunders persisted in focusing his attention on me. "I'm glad about that, Janey. It means I may have the opportunity of driving you and Sally to Bussum one day, and showing you over the studios there. We could have lunch in the Grand Gooiland in Hilversum, which isn't far away. How about it?"

"We already have our holiday planned out," Sally answered for me. "I'm afraid we won't have time to go to Bussum with you."

"I would rather like to look over the studios!" I demurred. "Unlike you, Sally, I have never visited one, and I think it would be interesting!"

"In that case, I shall arrange a visit for you," decided Saunders, looking pleased.

If I hadn't been put out by the way both Mike and Dirk were concentrating their attention on Sally, I would not have replied as I had, but the fact that Oliver Saunders was singling me out for attention was balm to my pride, and even if I did not find him particularly attractive, I felt flattered at being asked out by a well-known personality.

"I'll look forward to it!" I smiled at him, ignoring the look of annoyance that flitted briefly across Sally's face and the somewhat disapproving look Dirk shot in my direction.

"I'll be in touch about the arrangements later." Saunders pushed back his chair and stood up. "I'm sorry I have to leave now, but I have a business appointment I can't afford to miss. See you folks at the rehearsal this afternoon." He nodded to his colleagues.

"You won't see me!" Natasha replied. "Edward is entertaining a party of business acquaintances at the Amsterdam Hilton this evening. He has commanded my presence as hostess," she grimaced. "It will be deadly dull, but business is business, and a wife's duty is by her husband's side when it comes to that."

"I'll lay two to one you are only playing the dutiful wife because you will get a diamond thank you from him!" Saunders retorted nastily. "Will you take me on, Natasha?"

Bob Thorpe, the director, grinned.

"Natasha never gambles against a certainty. Make it the other way around and you might have a taker."

Natasha's lips tightened. It was plain she didn't like being made fun of, and Saunders knew this.

Without replying, she stubbed her cigarette in the ashtray with an angry gesture, and turned from them to pick up a slim, envelope-shaped handbag from the table. She opened it, took out a gold powder compact and a lipstick, and deftly touched up her makeup.

At the same time I delved into my bulging shoulder bag for the key to my room, which I had forgotten to drop into the reception box before going out for my morning stroll with Mike.

"Good heavens!" Oliver Saunders paused behind me and cast an amused glance down at the bag, as Mike had done the previous evening. "What all do you carry around in that thing?"

"Everything bar the kitchen sink!" grinned Mike.

"Everything that I don't want pinched by magpie chambermaids!" I was stung to retort. "Last night my belongings were given the once-over when I was down in the dining room, so now I am making certain that I leave nothing in the room for her to get her grubby little paws on!"

"Have you spoken to the management about this?" asked Dirk sharply.

"What's the use?" I shrugged. "I would be given a smooth apology, but I doubt if they would speak to the girl. Even here, domestic staff won't be easy to come by, and it isn't as if anything was stolen, although she managed to rip the side seams of my rag doll's dress with her clumsy handling of it."

"Chambermaids are the same the world over," remarked Natasha. "You have to accept the fact that they will use your perfumes and cosmetics, and even try on your coats and dresses if they get the chance."

I gave a shudder of distaste.

"I don't like the idea of a stranger trying on my clothes."

"Neither do I," said Sally. "Fortunately, I

must have a different girl from you. Nothing of mine has been interfered with."

Van der Woude opened his mouth to say something, but changed his mind as Saunders, passing behind Sally's chair, placed a hand on her shoulder and gave her an affable squeeze, saying:

"It's seven thirty you have to leave tomorrow, isn't it? If you like," he looked down at her, "I shall give you a ring and make sure you get up in time!"

"You needn't bother," said Sally sharply, wriggling from his clasp. "The hotel has an early call service."

"It was only a suggestion." He ignored her tone of rebuff. "I hope you both have a nice time tomorrow, and I shall be in touch with you about the Bussum arrangement later on. Ciao for now!"

He walked away and a few moments later his colleagues followed him, except for Natasha, who waited until the others had left the hotel before she too excused herself.

Sally rubbed her shoulder where Saunders had gripped it.

"I can't stand that man!" she said angrily. "He gives me the creeps! He can't keep his hands to himself, and I hate being pawed like that.

"Janey!" she glared across the table at me. "You shouldn't have accepted his invitation. He will think you are encouraging him, and he isn't the type to take no for an answer without a struggle."

"Don't be silly, Sally," I laughed. "What harm is there in being shown round some studios? After all, you and Mike will be there to chaperone me!"

"I didn't notice that crowd here last night," said Mike. "Are they staying in the Collenius?"

"Thank goodness, no," replied Sally. "They dropped in for a coffee, saw me sitting here on my own, and had to join me. Or rather, Saunders and Bob Thorpe and the others asked if they could sit here. Natasha was none too keen, until she heard Saunders try to wheedle me into giving him a mention in my next program. After that she tried to do the same."

"How are you feeling now, Sally?" asked Mike. "You still look a bit pale."

"I'm feeling a lot better," she assured him. "In fact, I think I've got over the turn, which is just as well, with the wedding tomorrow."

"Do you think you feel fit enough to go to the seaside?" he cajoled. "Scheveningen is only a tram ride away. We could lunch there and have a stroll along the dunes. The sea air will bring the color back to your cheeks."

"My car is parked at the back of the hotel," said van der Woude, who had stayed with us after the TV crowd had gone. "I am sure you would prefer the comfort of a car to a tram, wouldn't you?" He eyed Sally hopefully.

Mike's expression registered annoyance.

"If I had had any sense," he muttered, "I would have arranged to pick up the car I have hired for the wedding this morning, instead of this evening. Mike took mine to drive back to Anna's last night."

Sally looked at Dirk consideringly and finally said, lightly teasing, "Are you lending us the car, or are you coming with us as well?"

"I was hoping you would ask me along!" He grinned back at her.

"The car weighs in your favor. I think we shall let you come with us. What do you say, Janey?" she smiled.

I managed to hide the delight I felt at Sally's suggestion as I nodded agreement, and Mike could not go against our decision without appearing boorish, although from the expression I surprised on his face, I didn't think he was too pleased. He must have been aware, as I was, that in van der Woude he had a rival for Sally's attention, and with Sally playing up to both of them, as she was at present, neither could guess which of them she preferred.

## Chapter 7

Dirk pointed out that although it was a warm day, there was always a breeze at the coast, and he advised Sally and me to go up to our rooms to fetch a coat or a cardigan, while he went to the car park to get his car and drive it to the front door for us.

On our way to the lift, Sally scolded me once more for encouraging Oliver Saunders, but I pointed out to her that I was used to looking after myself, and for that matter I was immune to the charms other women saw in the TV star.

"It's just a piece of holiday fun," I told her, "and something to brag about to the other staff nurses when I get home. The ward sister is a fan of his, and it will be amusing to see her face when I tell her I was asked out by her hero!"

We went to our rooms, and I took time to put on fresh makeup and tidy my hair, which I tied back from my forehead with a narrow chiffon scarf whose blue matched the blue of my eyes. I couldn't compete with Sally for looks, but I could at least make the most of myself, and a critical glance in the mirror told me that today I was looking my best.

Sally was waiting for me outside her bedroom door with a thick white cardigan slung over her arm.

"I'm glad Dirk could come with us," she confided as we took the lift to the ground floor. "Someone always feels odd man or woman out in a threesome, don't you think?"

Someone could even feel odd woman out in a foresome, I thought, especially in this particular foursome, but Sally was looking so pleased about the afternoon's arrangements, I kept my thoughts to myself.

When Dirk drove up to the entrance to the hotel, Mike stepped forward, opened the back passenger door and ushered Sally into the car, before opening the front passenger door and indicating to me that that was where I was to sit, while he went to sit beside Sally in the back.

Dirk's eyebrows raised the merest fraction at this maneuver, but he smiled at me as if he was genuinely pleased that it was I and not Sally who was seated by his side.

I was fumbling with the seat belt, trying to find out how to adjust it, when he gently took the ends from my hands and clicked them into place, at the same time saying, "Is your wrist still paining you, Janey? I should have asked about it earlier."

"No, not really." I shook my head. "It was a bit stiff first thing this morning, but that soon wore off. I'm one of the lucky people whose skin heals quickly, although there is still some discoloration from the bruising. That is why I am wearing a long-sleeved blouse," I added as he glanced down at my wrist. "The marks look worse than they feel, and I shall keep them covered until they fade a little more."

While Mike and Sally chattered behind us, Dirk remained silent for a time, concentrating on maneuvering the car along the street, which was so narrow in places that at times we had to mount the pavement to get past parked vans. On one occasion, the side of our car was only inches from the plate glass window of a florist's shop.

I gasped with delight as we were forced to a standstill at this point, when the local dustcart came to a halt ahead of us, and wound down my window to have a better view of the blooms.

"I hope we manage to get a move on, before Janey gets out of the car to buy herself a bunch of those roses!" Sally tapped Dirk's shoulder. "She is flower mad! That is another of the reasons we came to Holland at this time of year."

"In that case, she will have the time of her life at Keukenhof," Dirk told her, but his eyes, looking in the driving mirror, were studying my reflection, not hers, as he continued:

"I hope I shall be free to go with you on that excursion as well."

"I thought you were in Holland on business?" said Mike. "What line are you in?"

I awaited Dirk's answer with interest. Although he had asked Sally and me a great deal about ourselves, and I had told him quite a lot about my background and my ambitions, he had said very little about himself, apart from the fact that he was of Dutch ancestry and had been born in Scotland.

"In my line, I find it is sometimes possible to combine business and pleasure," he replied lightly. "My base is in London, but I have been working over here for several weeks on a special project.

"Look, Janey! There's the Peace Palace!" Smoothly he switched attention from himself. "As a Scot, you might be interested to know that it was Dunfermline's Andrew Carnegie who contributed £300,000 toward the cost of the building, which incidentally is well worth a visit when you are here."

The streets had broadened out, and now we were driving along a spacious boulevard with attractive parklands on either side. In a remarkably short space of time we had reached the coast, where the blue gray waters of the North Sea rolled in across the sands. Looking toward the horizon, I had the strange feeling that we were below sea level and that the waters were about to take over.

I remarked to Dirk how I felt, and he laughed.

"That is a feeling the Dutch themselves have had for a very long time. More than half the population of the Netherlands lives on land which could be flooded at high tide, if there weren't protective dykes, and a fifth of the country is actually below sea level."

"The Lord made heaven and earth, but the Dutch made Holland!" Mike quoted from the back seat. "You would need to be fond of water, to live here!"

Dirk found a parking place near the Kurhaus, and we got out of the car and strolled along the broad esplanade with its hotels and discotheques on one side, and on the other, the extensive sand dunes and the ever-rolling sea, looking for what Dirk called a pancake house where we could have a light lunch.

Sally decided that it would not be wise to eat much, and she contented herself with a cup of coffee and a salad sandwich. However, I couldn't resist sampling a cheese pancake, and Mike and Dirk followed my example.

"I do hope it will be warm and sunny like this for Tim's wedding!" I remarked as I looked across the promenade at the sunlit sands.

"It's bound to be," said Mike. "My country bones tell me that the weather is set fair for the next few days."

"Mike, what are you going to do when you go back home?" I asked him. "Have you decided if you want to join forces with your father on his farm, or try for a manager's job with one of the Angus estates?"

"For a time, I thought I might like to work in New Zealand and see what the prospects are like out there."

"New Zealand?" Sally, who had been chatting

with Dirk, broke off her conversation with him to interrupt Mike. "That's the other side of the world!"

"So what?" he challenged her. "It's good farming country."

She seemed quite taken aback as she stuttered, "But Mike! You told me you had been offered a manager's job at a farm in Hampshire —one that has a Fresian herd! If you took that one you would be near enough to London to commute."

"What would I want to commute to London for?" he asked innocently. "Has it some special attraction for me?"

"Of course!" I replied mischievously. "I live there! Yes, I agree with Sally. If you have been offered this job definitely, I think you should take it—for my sake! It would be wonderful for me to get out of town and stay in real countryside every once in a while!"

Mike grinned across at Dirk.

"That's what I call being self-centered, don't you? All the same," he continued thoughtfully, "Janey has helped me make some of my major decisions for a long time, and she has usually been right. Do you think I should continue to let her run my life for me?"

"I think it is high time you made your own decisions, Mike Russell!" Sally said sharply. "Janey won't always be at your beck and call."

Sally and Mike continued to discuss his future prospects as we left the pancake house. Following them across to the sand dunes, I guessed, with an odd twinge of regret, that Sally would only have to say the word, and from now on she could be Mike's decision maker.

I looked thoughtfully after her as she linked her arm through Mike's while they walked slowly along the sands ahead of us. Was she as interested in my brother's friend as he had always been in her, or was she merely enjoying his company more than usual because she was on holiday and, as she herself had said, it was nice to have a handsome young man in tow to look after her in a foreign land? I couldn't be sure, any more than I could be sure that the odd, provocative remark she directed to Dirk from time to time was because she wanted to tease Mike, or perhaps even screen from him the fact that she was beginning to find him more attractive than heretofore, or because she wanted to keep Dirk dangling on the end of her line as well.

If my own feelings had not been involved, I might have found the situation amusing. I might even have found some opportunity to ask her if she was genuinely attracted to either man, but as it was, I was afraid I might be given an answer I did not want to hear.

Yet in spite of the emotional undercurrents, I enjoyed the afternoon. Dirk was fun to be with, and I discovered he had a similar sense of humor to my own, a similar attitude as to how one can enjoy oneself. While Mike and Sally were content to sit down on the sand and enjoy the sunshine and chatter to each other, he and I joined in a game of baseball of sorts, with a group of youngsters to whom Dirk had casually flung back the ball which had landed at his feet.

After half an hour I was exhausted, and I flopped down breathlessly on the sand beside Sally, who looked at my flushed face and disheveled hair and shook her head.

"If only the children in your ward could see you now!" she chaffed me. "They would think you were one of themselves, and not the big bad wolf who makes them swallow nasty medicines and the like!"

Mike agreed.

"You look fourteen and not twenty-four, Janey, my love! A female Peter Pan, lost in the Never Never Land!"

"Don't say that!" I spoke with irritation. "I don't want to be caught up forever in the same whirligig of time! I want—" I stopped abruptly.

I had been about to say, "I want to be taken for twenty-four! I want to be seen to be a mature woman, a woman a man could fall in love with and want to marry. I want to have children of my own, and not to be considered a child myself!" but such an outburst would have embarrassed Mike and Dirk, and Sally too.

"Yes?" prompted Dirk. "What is it you want from life, Janey?"

He stood looking down at me, and to give myself time to think up a suitable reply, I scrambled to my feet, vigorously brushed the sand from my slacks and blouse, and said lightly:

"I am not sure what I may want later on, but right now I would settle for a long, cool drink!"

Our glances met, and from the expression in his eyes I knew he was aware that I had not said what had been on the tip of my tongue to say earlier, but tactfully he did not challenge my statement.

Instead, he glanced at his watch, and agreed that it was definitely afternoon tea time.

"It can't be!" exclaimed Sally. "We have been here no time at all!"

"Dirk is right," confirmed Mike, glancing at his own watch. "The afternoon has flown past!"

He rose to his feet and dusted the fine grit from his trousers, while I opened my bag to find a comb to tidy my hair.

Sally held up her arms for Mike to help her to stand up, but Dirk made a sudden move toward her, as if he felt it was time he had his share of her company.

As he lurched forward, he managed to knock my still-open bag from my clasp, and to my consternation all its contents were scattered over the sand.

Dirk exclaimed apologetically as he bent down to retrieve them, but I was furious at his carelessness as I tried to shake the grit from my various possessions, and especially furious when I discovered that my favorite lipstick had lost its cap and was no longer usable since it was ingrained with sand.

"Janey, I am very sorry!" Dirk repeated ruefully. "When we get back to The Hague, I shall buy you another one."

"I hope you haven't lost anything?" asked Sally anxiously. "Things get buried so easily in sand. You had better check."

"Everything is here," I replied crossly, while Dirk opened the first-aid kit and the spectacle case which held my sunglasses, and vigorously blew the sand out of them.

I opened the small jewel case, which had been the first object I had retrieved, and made sure that the gold topaz necklet and matching bracelet which it contained were unharmed.

"What attractive pieces!" exclaimed Dirk admiringly as he peered over my shoulder into the box. "Family heirlooms?"

"They belonged to my grandmother," I replied, snapping the case shut and handing it to Dirk, who was carefully replacing each item into the shoulder bag. "The topaz was her favorite gem stone. It is mine too, for that matter."

"Are you sure that's the lot?" His frowning gaze searched the area of sand around us.

"Quite sure," I nodded.

"Surely you don't think Janey could stuff another item into that pouch of hers?" grinned Mike.

"She managed to stuff quite a large rag doll into it yesterday," replied Dirk, making sure that the catch was firmly fastened before handing the bag back to me.

"Talking of rag dolls," he continued in an offhand tone. "Apart from the one you wanted so

102

badly to buy at the market, and didn't, you don't happen to have a double, do you?"

I gaped at him in surprise.

"What made you ask that?"

Before van der Woude could answer me, Mike uttered an amused snort. "I should hope not!" he interjected cheekily. "One of Janey is quite enough!"

With that, he took hold of Sally's arm, to escort her back along the promenade to where Dirk had parked the car. Dirk automatically followed suit by taking my arm, but his grip was more that of a policeman taking a prisoner into custody than the casual arm link of a friend, and the frown which lingered on his face gave me the uncomfortable feeling that there was something about me which he found puzzling, and which he didn't like.

He was silent as we drove back to The Hague, and even during the meal, which we ate in the Italian restaurant not far from the Collenius, he seemed absorbed with his own thoughts. It was as if he had something on his mind which troubled him, and his off-hand responses to my attempts at conversation with him contrasted with the cheerful flow of banter Mike and Sally were exchanging with each other.

When we had finished the snack, the men walked back to the hotel with Sally and me, and lingered for a few minutes of casual chit-chat in the reception lounge.

Finally Mike decided that it was time to leave.

"I shall call for you at, say quarter past seven,

tomorrow morning," he announced. "That will give us a little extra time, in case of holdups."

He gave me a quick, brotherly kiss and hug, before turning to Sally, with whom he repeated the procedure, but in her case the kiss was not so brotherly, and the embrace was more protracted.

"Sleep well, Sally," he smiled at her. "Sweet dreams."

Dirk van der Woude did not attempt to follow the kiss and hug routine, but he wished us a pleasant good night, following this with a surprising warning.

"Don't forget to lock your doors and windows securely before you get into bed," he said. "You are not at home, you know."

"We aren't exactly innocents abroad, Dirk," retorted Sally in a peeved voice.

"Yes, I know that." He smiled. "But it is always best to be careful."

His attention switched to me.

"I hope there will be no disturbances outside your windows or your door tonight, and that the resident pop group who were ogling you as they passed us just now don't decide to serenade you!"

His tone was lighthearted, but there was no hint of laughter in his eyes as he was speaking, although he continued his raillery by adding, "I am the only one you must allow to do that!"

I knew he meant nothing by this remark and was merely trying to emulate the banter Sally and Mike were enjoying with each other, but I could not help wishing that he had meant what he said. And it was of his teasing remark about serenading me, rather than about the warning he had expressed before it, that I was thinking after he and Mike waved us good night as they left the hotel and I trailed after Sally to the lift.

To round off a day which had been a mixture of ups and downs, and not at all what Sally and I had originally planned, the telephone rang seconds before I was about to slip into bed.

"It's Sally, Janey. Mike has just called me to say that there was a message from Tim waiting for him when he returned to his flat."

"There is nothing wrong!" I gasped anxiously.

"Not in the way you are thinking," she replied wryly, "Although you will welcome the news as little as I did!

"The civil marriage ceremony has been put forward by half an hour, which means we shall have to be dressed and on our way by six thirty!"

"Oh, no!" I groaned. "Have you told the night porter to alter the early morning call time?"

"Yes, I have, but the way I feel now," she yawned, "I am liable to sleep through any alarm call, so Janey," she pleaded, "make sure I am awake in time!"

"I'll try," I mumbled, equally sleepily. "Good night."

I crawled into bed, smiling to myself as I decided that Mike had got in touch with Sally about the change in my brother's wedding plans, rather than with me, because it gave him an excuse to have another chat with her, and I fell asleep with the thought that it was highly probable that when Mike himself married, I would only be a bridesmaid at the wedding, and not the bride, as a number of people, my own parents included, expected me to be.

## Chapter 8

At five o'clock my alarm clock woke me from a restless sleep. I yawned and stretched and extended a lazy hand to switch off the shrilling bell. No sooner had I done so than my early morning call came through on the telephone, to make sure that I didn't fall asleep again.

There was a frosty chill in the air, and I shivered as I got out of bed and crossed the room to pull aside the curtains.

The morning was clear and golden bright, with a white rime reflecting the dawn sun. Birds, hidden from my view by the leafy foliage of the limes and the thick purple plumes of the lilacs in the garden below, were caroling sweetly, delighted by the promise of a sunny day ahead, and I too felt like singing as I flung open the window and inhaled a deep breath of the frost-sharp, lilac-scented air.

There was no doubt that the sun was going to shine for Anna today, and I was glad for her, and glad for Tim, that this should be so.

"This is my lovely day!" Softly I sang the lyric from Vivien Ellis's delightful "Bless The Bride," as I went to the bathroom to turn on the shower, and I continued to sing to myself as I stepped under the invigorating spray of water, which banished the last remnants of sleep from me.

I dressed quickly, put on a light film of makeup, brushed out my hair so that it hung in a gleaming pageboy roll over my shoulder, and finally clipped on the lovely topaz necklet and bracelet which went so well with my sherry gold dress.

It seemed strange to be wearing a long, formal gown at this early hour, but Anna had written to tell me that it was the custom in her hometown to dress up like this for a wedding. I surveyed myself critically in the long mirror, and my reflection told me that I looked elegant in my simple, shirtwaist-style dress, with its broad belt emphasizing my tiny waist.

Tim had warned me that the wedding would be an all-day affair, and quite unlike what we were used to at home.

It would start with the early civil ceremony in the Burgermeistry, followed by the church ceremony. Then would come the wedding breakfast. In the afternoon there would be a champagne reception not only for close friends of the family, but also for the local dignitaries. This would be followed in the evening by the wedding feast and dancing, and since the festivities could well go on until long past midnight, Tim had advised

Sally and me to pack an overnight case, in the event of our feeling too tired, after all the fun, to face the three-hour drive back to The Hague. In this event, Anna's parents had provisionally booked a room for us in a small hotel in their village.

I was putting my makeup bag into my hold-all when there was a knock at the door. I opened it, and Sally stood outside, looking very sophisticated and lovely in a long dress of fine pink gabardine, a short fur jacket draped over her shoulders, her handbag and overnight case in one hand.

"Good! You're ready," she smiled at me. "Mike telephoned me a few minutes ago to say he had arrived and was waiting in the lobby."

She waited at the door while I snapped my case shut, took my tan suede jacket from the wardrobe, and carefully wriggled into it.

"Isn't it nice that the sun is shining for the bride," said Sally as I followed her to the lift. "Tim was so worried that it might not."

"He wants everything to be perfect for his Anna," I sighed. "She is a lucky girl, having him dote on her the way he does!"

We stepped from the lift and Mark came forward to meet us, and to congratulate us both on being ready in good time.

The streets were almost devoid of traffic as we made our way to join the main road out of town. In the early sunlight, with its white covering of frost, the city looked fresh and lovely. In the parkland which bordered the road leading to the motorway for Amsterdam, deer were enjoying the dew-fresh grass, and the May foliage of the trees was so softly green it seemed almost unreal.

"This is the right time to view any country," said Mike as we sped along the motorway. The trees gave way to more open country and views of windmills and cows placidly chewing the lush vegetation beside inlets of water. Then came the fields upon fields of tulips, which stretched as far as the eye could see, and from the built-up roadway, it was as if priceless carpets of rich scarlets and golds and yellows and pinks, almost eye-searing, so vivid were the colors, had been spread out especially for our enjoyment.

If there hadn't been so much of interest to look at, the steady drumming of the tires on the road surface as we raced along would have lulled me to sleep.

The miles sped past, and soon we reached Amsterdam, with its tall, narrow, gabled houses, and its canals which reflected back the houses, and the elm trees which lined their banks. It seemed a most intricate city to find one's way through, but Mike knew the route and was even able to indicate to us some of the places of interest which we drove past, until we came to the tunnel which went under the water and led from the city on to the road which would eventually take us past the Ijsslmeer and on to Friesland.

I noticed a change in the scenery as we drove northward. There were more small villages; villages with names which I recognized, like Volendaam, and Edam, famous for its cheeses, and we even glimpsed some women in picturesque local costumes already out and about their daily business.

Villages slipped past with a mesmeric regularity until we came to the broad dyke which separates the area of water once known as the Zuyder Zee, now called the Ijsslmeer, from the sea.

It was an uncanny experience, racing along this straight, endless-seeming man-made barrier, with the North Sea washing against the dam on one side, and on the other, the placid blue waters of the new freshwater lake sparkling in the brilliant sunshine. I felt that we were isolated from the rest of mankind, with gulls as the only other living beings to be seen, and no other traffic on the road, except a single distant car which had followed in our wake since we left the Amsterdam tunnel.

Mike and Sally, in the front seat, were chatting lightly to each other, and seemed to have forgotten my existence. I felt lonely and sad and strangely uneasy as I stared out of the window. So still was the air, so isolated the lonely road with only infinity in front of it—for there was now no sign of land ahead—that we seemed to have reached the edge of the world. At any moment my imagination pictured us driving over the edge of the earth into eternity.

I shivered violently at this macabre thought.

Mike noticed my movement in the driving mirror.

"Are you cold, Janey?" he asked. "Shall I switch the heater on?"

"It's all right, Mike, thanks. I was merely thinking what a spooky ride this is, with the road stretching forward into the horizon of sky, and nothing on either side of us except water, and more water! Is it always as quiet as this?"

"It is early yet for traffic. At peak times it can be very busy, but I have never thought of it as lonely when I've driven over the dyke on my own, late at night or early in the morning. When you are driving you don't notice the scenery to the same extent. All you see in the main is the road ahead, and any following traffic in the driving mirror."

He put up his hand to adjust the mirror as he spoke, and added, frowning, "That car behind us is beginning to annoy me. It has been on our tail all the way from Amsterdam."

"What's unusual about that?" asked Sally. "I gather that this is the only way to get to Friesland from there, and I'm sure the engineers had more people than you in mind when they built it," she teased.

Mike's frown remained.

"I've given him lots of chances to get past me. I hate to have someone sit on my tail, mile after mile."

"Why not slow down to a crawl, and then the driver will have to pass us," I suggested.

"We want to arrive at Anna's place as quickly as possible," he said impatiently, "and we won't do that if we start to dawdle. No," he decided. "I think I shall do the opposite!"

With that he pressed his foot harder down on the accelerator, so that the speedometer needle rose steadily beyond 120 to the 130-kilometer mark, to hover eventually around 150 kilometers.

Mike grinned happily as the following car became a smaller and smaller speck in his driving mirror, but I was thankful when we reached the end of the breakwater and drove on to firm land again. I had had uncomfortable thoughts about what could have happened had we had a blowout at high speed, and I hadn't fancied spinning around and around over the carriageway and perhaps even crashing over the dyke and falling into the cold water of the North Sea!

We turned right, away from the coast road, and again there was a dramatic change in the scenery as we raced toward Bolsward and the village beyond it, which was Anna Starke's hometown.

Here herds of cows, their black-and-white hides looking velvet smooth in the sunlight as they munched the green grass in the low-lying fields, replaced the endless carpets of the tulip fields around Amsterdam, and gradually the peacefulness of this bucolic scenery soothed away the malaise I had felt when driving along the dyke.

We passed through Bolsward, a pleasant town, with a fine town hall and several attractive old churches, and a few miles farther on we turned off into a narrow side road which led along a canal to Apelward, Anna's hometown.

Mike drove direct to the Park Hotel, where the Starkes had booked a room where Sally and I could freshen ourselves up after our long drive, and also, if we so desired, spend the night when the wedding celebrations ended.

We carried our cases up to our room, freshened up our makeup, put on the pretty straw hats which matched our dresses, and went to rejoin Mike, who was waiting beside the car to take us to the Starke farmhouse on the outskirts of the village.

When Mike stopped the car in the yard near the front entrance, I was overcome with an unexpected fit of the jitters.

In order to give myself time to pull myself together, I made no move to leave the car, but sat staring out of the window at the pleasant tiled-roof building, the top of which was reflected in the calm waters of the nearby canal.

A small boat was moored to the tow path, and a duck, followed by a retinue of tiny brown ducklings, paddled around it. Beyond the farmhouse, the spread of green fields shimmered in the golden light, and only in the deepest shade were there traces of the overnight rime.

This tranquil scene had the desired effect of soothing my nervousness, so that by the time Mike opened the car door for me and I had carefully readjusted the tilt of my broad-brimmed hat, I was myself again.

Mike slammed the door shut behind me, and

taking Sally and me by the arm he escorted us to the door.

The closing of the car door must have alerted those inside of our arrival, for before we had moved forward more than a few paces, the front door opened and a slim, pretty girl, dressed in a white bridal gown, came out into the sunshine, holding her arms out in welcome.

"Janey!" she smiled at me.

"Anna!"

I could feel moisture gather in the corner of my eyes as we smiled at each other, and I blinked it away.

"I have been longing to meet you!"

We spoke simultaneously, giggled simultaneously, and sniffed back an emotional tear simultaneously.

Looking at Anna, I knew my brother had made a wise choice. There were laughter wrinkles at the corners of the bride-to-be's cornflower-blue eyes, dimples in her rose-pink cheeks, and she radiated happiness. Also from what my brother had told me of how she coped in helping her parents on the farm as well as teaching English, and being a cordon bleu cook, I knew she was more than just a pretty face.

By this time the other members of the family had come spilling out of the house to meet us.

Mrs. Starke was a small, plumpish, pretty woman, the mirror of what Anna would look like in twenty years. She gave me a warm hug of welcome and said how pleased they all were that I had been able to come to Apelward.

Mr. Starke was a giant of a man, with still-blond hair, ruddy cheeks and twinkling eyes. He caught my hand in a vise-like grip, grinned, and bent down to kiss me welcome, extending a similar greeting to Sally.

Mrs. Starke led the way into the house and we stood, chattering like magpies for about ten minutes, until Anna's bridesmaid, a dainty doll-like girl, not unlike Anna in appearance, whispered to the bride that it was time to go upstairs and put on their chaplets and the veil.

After they had gone, Mrs. Starke plied me with eager questions about her daughter's future home, and then Mr. Starke, without preamble, asked me if my parents were pleased that their son was going to take home a foreign bride.

"They are happy because he is happy, just as you are happy because Anna is happy, even though she is going to live so far from you," I assured them. "They are looking forward to meeting her, and they will make her as much at home in Scotland as you have made Tim at home here."

"Anna won't find the place where she is going to live so very different from here, in some respects," said Sally. "She may find the mountains somewhat awesome at first, and the Aberdeen Angus herds a whit different from the Friesians you breed here, but in the springtime she will thinks she is back in Holland, for we have a thriving bulb industry, and the fields of daffodils and tulips will remind her of home."

While we were talking to the Starkes, Mike

had slipped off to fetch Tim, who was staying in the village with one of Anna's cousins. Sally and I were given coffee and introduced to more new arrivals who crowded in to the lovely living room of the farmhouse. With its timbered ceiling, its broad window ledges covered with pots of green house plants which trailed down to the floor and spread up the walls right to the rafters, we seemed to be in a pleasant arbor rather than in a house.

Shortly before nine thirty, Mike returned with Tim, who looked very handsome in his wedding suit, although he grinned self-consciously as he entered the room carrying the bride's bouquet of cream roses and trails of tiny brown and cream orchids. He had with him also an enormous box of white carnations, and these were distributed to the guests.

Although Mike attended to the bridesmaid, his eyes constantly strayed to where Sally and I were standing. I nudged her and whispered, smiling, "I was right about Mike, wasn't I? You are the one he is interested in!"

Sally blushed and told me not to be silly, but her eyes were sparkling, and she looked almost as radiant as the bride as we fell in line to enter the cars which would follow the bridal carriage to the Burgermeistry.

When the civil ceremony was over, we walked to the charming small church which stood on the corner of the chestnut-tree-lined square directly opposite the town hall, where the religious ceremony was to take place.

The chestnut trees, their fan-shaped leaves spread out like holders under the tall white candles of their flower spikes, made a natural canopy for the bridal party as they approached the church steps, and the old church itself, with its family pews linked together with coats of arms, its Gothic vaulting covered with frescoes of biblical scenes, was the ideal setting for the wedding service.

My impression of that hour was of flowers and smiles and sunlight and joyful voices joining in sincerity to sing the wedding hymn.

Tim and Anna looked so happy and so delighted with each other as they walked from the church that once more I felt tears prick my eyelids. I wasn't the only one thus affected, for I saw the bride's mother and aunts with tears sparkling in their eyes, and even Sally dabbed surreptitiously at her cheeks with a wisp of lace handkerchief.

Bells were ringing, passing motor cars hooted their congratulations as photographers stood taking pictures of the bride and groom, the bridesmaid and the wedding guests, and there was much laughter as some of the younger set struck up ludicrous poses.

The square was filled with the sound of laughter and voices as people left the church to stroll to the hotel not far away, where the several receptions, starting with the wedding breakfast, were to be held.

I was amused to see how Mike skillfully contrived to arrange things so that he could look after Sally as well as the bridesmaid.

I myself had been taken under the wing of Jan Stuyvesant, another of Anna's cousins. Like her father, he was a tall, broad-shouldered man, with blue eyes, and a great bellow of a laugh which could be heard the length and breadth of the square. Stuyvesant had ogled me from the moment we had been introduced in the Starkes' living room, and from then on he had amused me, not only by his joviality, but by the firm way he kept at bay the other young men who had made a beeline for my company.

Jan spoke excellent English, but with an American accent which he had acquired while living in Vermont for several months, and I found it less of a strain to converse with him than to attempt to keep up a flow of my stilted Dutch with the other guests who did not speak English to any extent.

## Chapter 9

The wedding breakfast was a protracted affair,
with as much chatting as eating. Many of the
guests had not seen each other for some time,
and for them the occasion was a pleasant re-
union.

Anna somehow found an opportunity to come
and talk to me privately. She was eager to be
friendly, eager to know how I was enjoying myself, wanted to know if I liked her country, and
was looking forward to hearing about the new
home she would be going to, from a woman's
point of view.

"Tim has described the house and the garden
and the district to me, Janey, but there are
things which he hasn't talked about, because
they don't interest him, as a man."

I answered her questions as best I could, but
so many people wanted to talk to her, she reluctantly had to go and chat with her other friends
and elderly relatives who had traveled quite a
distance to attend the wedding.

People seemed to keep coming and going all the time, and at one point Sally whispered she was sure there were a few gate crashers come to enjoy the feast, the room became so crowded.

Shortly before mid-day we noticed several of the guests slip away. Mike, who had been talking to the Starkes, came to tell us that there would be another reception in the afternoon, when he would see us again, but meantime he was going off to help Tim with some special ploy.

Although Jan Stuyvesant did not want to let me out of his sight, when Mike left Sally and I excused ourselves on the grounds that we were tired after our early start and would like to return to our room in the Park Hotel for a short rest.

It was very pleasant to stroll along the tree-shaded village high street, and refreshingly cool under the spreading boughs through which the sunlight scarcely penetrated. It had been an exceptionally hot day for so early in May, and Sally and I were glad that Mrs. Starke had had the forethought to arrange for us to have the room in the hotel, where we could go to rest, have a wash and freshen ourselves when we felt like getting away from the nonstop festivities.

"I have never been to a wedding like this before," yawned Sally when we entered the bedroom. "I am quite tired already. I don't know where the other guests get the energy to eat and drink and be merry without showing signs of wilting from such an early hour, especially when I am told we are still likely to be eating and drinking and making merry until well after midnight!"

"It is fun, isn't it?" I, too, stifled a yawn. "Anna is a dear, and so pretty! I'm not surprised Tim thinks the sun rises and sets on her. And they look so happy together." I sighed.

"I rather like your blond young cavalier," chuckled Sally. "Mike and I have been laughing at the way he commandeered you, and then proceeded to repel all other comers!"

I smiled.

"Jan is very pleasant and fun to be with. He only has to laugh and he makes you feel it is good to be alive. Not only that, he speaks English so effortlessly, I don't have to try and stutter my way through a conversation in my newly acquired Dutch."

"Wouldn't it be funny if you married a Dutch boy?" Sally grinned at me as she kicked off her shoes and wiggled her toes to loosen them up after their long confinement in their narrow leather sheaths.

"If there is going to be another wedding in the near future, Sally," I retorted, "it won't be mine, but I have a good idea whose it might be!"

Sally didn't reply to this quip, and I could not see her face to gauge her reaction to it, for she had turned her back to me and was pulling off her dress. She hung it carefully in the wardrobe before slumping on to the bed, closing her eyes and saying, with a complete disregard for my teasing, "I don't know about you, Janey, but I am going to take a catnap. Wake me up in half an hour, will you?"

Almost before I could reply, she had rolled on to her side and was fast asleep.

Although I too felt sleepy after our early start that morning, I was much too emotionally excited by my brother's wedding to be able to settle to rest. Instead of following Sally's example, I crossed the room, opened the french window, and went out to sit on the balcony which overlooked the village high street.

The hotel was on the shadowy side of the road, so it was pleasantly cool sitting there and looking down on to the green spreading branches of the chestnut trees, through which I caught an occasional glimpse of people passing along the street below.

Through the pattern of the leaves I could see the car in which Mike had driven us to Apleward parked near the entrance to the hotel, where he had left it when he had gone to fetch Tim and take him to the Starkes' farm in the bridal car.

Someone had festooned a garland of tulips over the wipers and the bonnet, to indicate that the car belonged to one of the wedding party, and I could see other cars similarly decorated parked on the other side of the road. In fact, the only car within range which did not have some kind of floral decoration was a dark green Audi, which was being driven slowly up the high street.

This car stopped in the middle of the road, a

few yards in front of Mike's car, and reversed to park immediately behind it and almost directly beneath the balcony on which I was sitting.

The driver got out, stepped forward to stare curiously at the garland on the bonnet of Mike's car, glanced across at the hotel entrance, appeared to hesitate as to what he wanted to do next, and eventually returned to the Audi, beside which he stood for a few seconds as if debating what his next step would be.

The stranger's movements were so odd that they made me pay more attention to him that I would normally have done.

From where I was, all I could see of the man was the top of his head, where short, curly gray hair surrounded the tanned bald patch above his crown.

I was about to look away when abruptly he put out his hand to grasp the car handle. Something about the gesture reminded me of a similar action I had seen recently, and I scowled, trying to recall the tantalizing memory which had surfaced momentarily, then gone as quickly as it had come. Yes, there had been something oddly familiar about the man's movement, but what?

I stood up quietly and craned over the railing of the balcony, in the hope of catching a clearer glimpse of the man's face before he entered his vehicle. But although he stood holding the handle for a little while longer, glancing up and down the road as if he was expecting to see someone he knew, the leafy foliage prevented me from getting a good look at his features, and

when he did eventually pull open the door and
bent down to enter the car, his movement was
so swift I caught the merest glimpse of his
profile and did not have time to register it, although I had a nagging suspicion that he was
someone I had seen before.

I stared after the departing Audi with a
frown. I was annoyed with myself for not being
able to think why the man, or perhaps only his
mannerism, should seem familiar, and I continued to gaze down the road long after the car had
disappeared from view.

Still frowning, I stepped back into the bedroom. Sally, roused by the sound of my footsteps
on the creaking broads by the window, opened
her eyes and glanced at me.

"What's wrong, Janey?" she inquired sleepily.
"You look worried."

It was on the tip of my tongue to tell her
about the man in the car and his strange behav-
ior, and how I thought I had recognized him,
but I bit back the words.

The last time I had told Sally I thought I had
recognized someone, in that instance the lad
who had tried to snatch my bag from me, she
had laughed and pointed out how silly I was.

This time she wouldn't only laugh, she would
tease me about my overvivid imagination, and
tell me how stupid I was being, letting a complete stranger upset me by his mysterious actions. And she would be right to tease me, I told
myself firmly. I was letting my imagination run
away with me these days. Lots of people

resemble other people and have similar manner-isms. I had been stupid to imagine anything sin-ister in the actions of the stranger I had spied on surreptitiously.

I was tired: I was naturally somewhat over-wrought with the excitement of Tim's wedding. I was also rather worried about Mike's friend-ship with Sally.

I was fond of Mike and I was fond of Sally. I knew that Mike, for all his tomfoolery, was a sen-sitive young man, and I also knew that Sally de-lighted in casual flirtations. In this case I hoped she wasn't merely stringing Mike along for the fun of it.

I was also on edge because of the emotional attraction Dirk wan der Woude had for me, and trying to tell myself it was ridiculous to think so much about a man I had known for barely forty-eight hours. But Dirk's face, his way of looking at me, the sudden brilliance of his smile, seemed to haunt me, so that I found myself comparing other men with him to their detri-ment.

It was only natural that the turmoil of my emotions should make me nervous and on edge, but it was verging on the ridiculous to be so much on edge that I started at shadows! It was high time I pulled myself together, I scolded myself.

"Well?" prompted Sally. "What was making you look so worried?"

"Worried?" I managed a natural laugh as I went on, with a shake of my head, "I wasn't looking worried, Sally. I was merely feeling an uncomfortable twinge at having eaten so much this morning."

"I thought you looked worried," she persisted, searching my face.

"Sally!" I protested. "Now it is you who are imagining things! What have I to look worried about? The sun is shining. I am enjoying Tim's wedding. I even have a dashing Dutchman dancing attendance on me, so what more could I want?"

Sally continued to look at me thoughtfully.

"Tell me the truth, Janey." She spoke slowly. "You aren't annoyed with me about Mike, are you? Are you quite sure that isn't what is upsetting you?"

I gaped at her, completely taken aback by her surmise.

"Why should I be annoyed about you and Mike, Sally? Believe me, I am delighted to see how well you two get on together, only—" I hesitated.

"Yes?" she rapped out.

"Sally, don't lead him on too far, please. I am very fond of Mike, as you know. He is like one of the family and I wouldn't like to see him hurt."

Sally's expression changed. It was as if I had taken a load off her mind.

"I wouldn't dream of hurting Mike." She smiled. "I am very fond of him too!"

She swung from the bed.

"Come on, Janey!" she said briskly. "Let's get

back to the festivities. My catnap has made a new woman of me!"

I sensed that it had been what I had said about Mike, rather than the few minutes of sleep she had snatched, which made Sally so eager to get back to the wedding party, and she lost no time in getting dressed again and pinning her decorative hat into position over her silky hair, so that we could hurry back to the reception rooms.

The afternoon session was even merrier and noiser than the morning one. Champagne flowed freely, and caviar and canapés were provided for the party, which now included a number of the town dignitaries and officials. This sumptuous reception was followed in the evening by a magnificent supper, at which everyone was personally received by the bride and groom and the rest of the bride's family, and Mike.

It wasn't until almost eleven o'clock that the ceremony of cutting the wedding cake took place, and after everyone had received a piece, there was dancing.

Jan Stuvyesant's dancing was as vigorous and hearty as his talk and his laughter, and he swung me around and around until I was certain I would collapse from dizziness and sheer exhaustion.

"Am I glad that the Starkes booked a room for us at the hotel!" muttered Sally when we had a brief moment together during a lull in the dancing. "I couldn't have faced the long drive back to The Hague after all this. In fact," she added, "I doubt if I'll even have the strength to walk down the road to the hotel!"

"That's all right. I shall carry you," grinned Mike, who had overheard her last remark. "But you mustn't give in yet! The last waltz is about to be announced, and you promised you would dance it with me."

While their guests were dancing to the strains of "Tales from the Vienna Woods," the bride and groom slipped unobtrusively from the room, and when the music came to an end, friends kissed and embraced each other and went to thank the bride's parents for their hospitality before they left the hall.

There were several other wedding guests staying at the Park Hotel, and as we emerged from the reception rooms into the street we joined forces and formed a laughing chain as we danced a conga down the road to our destination.

Mike and Jan boldly kissed Sally and me good night at the entrance to the hotel, reminding us, before they left, that they would be calling for us at nine o'clock the following morning.

Mr. and Mrs. Starke had invited Sally, Mike and me to join them for a mid-day snack before we left for The Hague, and Jan Stuyvesant had decided that since we would be in Apelward until luncheon, we might as well be shown something of the area during the morning.

Neither Sally nor I wasted much time in getting into bed. I was so exhausted I was sure that I would sleep through the noises of the alarm, which we had set for eight o'clock.

I was wakened long before eight, and it was not the alarm bell which roused me. It was a more primitive, intuitive alarm system which dragged me from the depths of sleep; an alarm system triggered off by an errie feeling of terror which made the hairs at the nape of my neck bristle and stand on end.

If I had been one of my pet cats, I would have arched my back and fluffed my tail and inhaled with an angry hiss, as they do when they are unexpectedly and frighteningly disturbed.

As it was, I lay still, feeling chilled to the marrow as I turned my eyes so that the window came into my line of vision, certain that the sound which had roused me had come from that direction.

As I stared through the glass, a dark shape on the balcony blotted out the moonlight, and again I heard the noise which had startled me into wakefulness—the grating sound of metal as the handle of the french window was slowly turned this way and that, in an attempt to open the lock.

I couldn't control the scream which rose to my throat. I sat up in bed with a jerk and fumbled on the bedside table for the heavy ashtray to use as a weapon to defend myself against the would-be intruder.

My shrill cry wakened Sally, who also sat up with a jerk.

"What's wrong?" she gasped.

I pointed to the window.

"Someone was trying to get in!"

We both stared at the moonlit rectangle, but now there was no dark shadow half obscuring the light, no sign of movement of any kind.

Sally muttered angrily, "There is no one there, Janey. You've been having a nightmare, and no wonder, after all the excitement."

I couldn't believe I had been dreaming. I had been sitting up in bed when I saw the menacing shape.

Sally settled back to sleep, but I slipped from my bed and tiptoed to the window to look out.

There was certainly no one on the balcony, and there was no one, from where I was standing with my face pressed against the glass, to be seen in the roadway below.

I drew the line at stepping out on to the balcony and peering over the railing, and so I did not spot the fingers of the man who was clinging to the concrete ledge; the stubby, broken-nailed fingers of the man with badly scarred hands, who dropped lightly to the ground and remained skulking in the shadows a mere fifteen feet below, before sliding away to the car which was parked around the corner.

Had I known of his presence, I would not have returned to bed so unconcernedly, telling myself that as usual Sally had been right, and I had had an unpleasant nightmare as a result of my overindulgence at the wedding feast. I pulled the sheet over my head and quickly fell asleep again.

# Chapter 10

I woke to the joyful sound of bells ringing. It was a pleasing, happy noise, and I closed my eyes again and lay back to enjoy the carillons and to think back to the events of the previous day.

In the brightness of daylight, the frightening nightmare which had roused me, terror stricken, in the small hours of the morning now seemed remote and unreal, and I felt ashamed at myself for the way in which I had startled Sally from her sleep and tried to convince her that what I had dreamed had actually happened.

"Up you get, you sleepyhead!" Sally's brisk voice interrupted my thoughts. "It's a glorious Sunday morning. Just look at the sunshine!"

She pulled the curtains back still further so that I could see the golden gleam on the red tiles of the roofs across the square, and the way the sunshine lit up the topmost candles of the flowering chestnuts in the street below.

"I've discovered that there is only one

bathroom on this floor," she went on, "so I am going to be first in the queue! Fortunately it is right next door to us, so I shall give a bang on the wall when I am about to leave, and you can be ready to pop in."

This arrangement worked well, and I managed to slip into the bathroom seconds ahead of a man who had been parading the corridor, waiting for a chance to get in.

When I returned to the bedroom, Sally, who was now dressed, greeted me crossly.

"Janey, I wish you wouldn't rake around in my case without asking me. I don't know what you were looking for, but you have managed to crumple the blouse which I was wanting to wear today, if the weather was hot. I have had to put on my cotton pullover instead!"

I looked at her in surprise.

"Sally, I didn't touch your case. Why should I?" I was equally annoyed with her for her suspicion that I would search through her things.

I was even more annoyed when, seconds later, I opened my own case to get my makeup kit, which I had locked in it, to discover that someone had been tampering with its contents as well, and had even unwrapped the box containing the malt Scotch whisky which I had brought as a present for Anna's father and also the box of rich Strathspey cake which I intended to give to her mother before leaving Apelward.

"It's a damned chambermaid who has been at it again!" I said furiously. "First in the Collenius, now here. Natasha was right, they are the same nosey lot everywhere!"

I dressed in the casual, rust-colored pants outfit which I had worn on the excursion to Scheveningen, carefully rewrapped the presents, muttering angrily the while, then waited for Sally to put the finishing touches of carmine to her lips, before we went down to the breakfast room.

Although the central table was set for the usual hearty Dutch breakfast of piled-up plates of wafer-thin cheeses and hams and sausages, and mounds of crusty rolls and rye breads, after the previous day's feasting neither of us was hungry, and a roll with honey with a cup of steaming black coffee sufficed.

Mike arrived before we had finished eating, and seconds later Jan Stuyvesant, so tall and broad-shouldered that he dwarfed everyone else in the room, breezed in to wish us a hearty good morning.

"I am glad the sun is still shining," he grinned at me. "I wanted you to see this area at its best!"

He continued to talk about his homeland while we all drank another cup of coffee, and from the way he spoke, I gathered that as far as he was concerned Friesland was Holland, or at least its most important state.

He had decided that we would do the morning tour in his car, and he was not the type of person one argued with, although I knew that Mike preferred driving to being driven.

Jan's car was a large, roomy American one, a Cadillac, and exactly the kind of car needed to accommodate his large person. It was also another sign of his pro-American bias, which I had detected in other ways the previous day.

Yesterday I had been too excited, too interested in all that was going on around me, and toward evening too tired to take in everything that Jan had told me about himself, but now, fortunately for me, he repeated his life story for Sally's benefit.

Apparently he was a direct descendant of the Peter Stuyvesant who had been born in Friesland in 1592. This Stuyvesant was the man who was considered to be the founder of New York, which he named New Amsterdam, and whose farm in Holland, Groet Bowerie, gave its name to the Bowery district of the greatest city in the United States.

Mike was sitting in the back seat of the Cadillac, one arm stretched along the top of the seat, the hand drooping over to touch Sally's shoulder. He gave my hair a gentle tug with his free hand, and as I looked around at him, he winked and said to Jan, "Your cousin Anna isn't by any chance related to that other famous Friesian, is she?"

"Who is that?" demanded Jan seriously.

"Mata Hari!" grinned Mike, with another wink in my direction.

Jan boomed with laughter, and his shoulders shook with such amusement that the car almost rocked over the central line of the road.

"Can you imagine little Anna playing the part of a dangerous, exotic woman spy?" he chuckled. "No! No! She is as open as our fields! There is nothing devious about her nature."

Jan had insisted in taking us to Friesland's capital, Leeuwarden, a stately looking city with narrow, gabled houses, Gothic spires and straight canals. To my untutored eye it looked similar to other Dutch towns we had passed through, but I couldn't hurt Jan's feelings by saying so.

It was different, however, in the fact that it had the largest cattle market in Europe, of which Jan was very proud, and it was where he said he would introduce me to *Us Mem*.

"*Us Mem?*" I looked at him, wondering if he was referring to a favorite relative, or a favorite local dish, for I had learned yesterday that Jan was a great trencherman who would sit and enjoy a hearty meal at any time of the day.

"*Us Mem?*" I repeated, "Is she a special friend of yours?"

Jan let out another mirthful bellow.

"*Ja!* A very special friend!"

He managed to squeeze his car into a parking space and we walked back to the center of the town.

"There she is!" He pointed to a bronze statue. "*Us Mem!* Our mother! The symbol of our prosperity!"

There, looking down at us from its place of honor in the center of the city, symbolizing the thriving local industry of dairy farming, was a

136

magnificent cow, its bronze hide gleaming in the morning sunshine, looking very much the monarch of all she surveyed.

After we had admired it, Jan rushed us along the street to see the bronze tablet which commemorates the fact that Leeuwarden was the first city to recognize the United States of America, and it dawned on me that it was because the area in which he lived had so many ties with the United States that he had a special soft spot for it.

Sally and I longed to linger and look at the shop windows with their entrancing displays of distinctive pottery and strange clocks in all shapes and sizes, but Jan, having shown us his two favorite sights, decided we had seen all that was necessary.

"Time for morning coffee!" he suggested, and once again his long-legged stride had me half running to keep up with him, as he led the way to a small, pleasant café in one of the narrow streets away from the main center.

Here, over seed cakes and Drabbel cookies, specialties of the area, while we drank black coffee with daubs of cream on top, Jan told me of his visit to the States.

"I spent over a year in Vermont." There was a trace of nostalgia in his voice as he spoke. "Most of the time at Burlington State University, but also several months working on the farm of some distant cousins.

"I learned a lot from them." His voice trailed

off, and for a moment he looked as if he was lost in a dream.

"You remind me of one of these cousins." He forced the dream away, and his blue-eyed, direct gaze swept over me. "Yes, you remind me very much of Marguerite, Janey. I thought that from the moment I set eyes on you, standing in the sunlight in the window of Uncle Willi's sitting room."

He continued to stare at me, giving me the eerie feeling that it was not really me he was seeing, but another girl with fair hair and blue eyes and a ready smile for his jokes—a girl whom, from the note of sadness I detected in his voice, he had loved, and for some reason, had had to leave.

I looked down into my coffee with unhappy eyes. Why did my role in life have to be as player of second fiddle when it came to attractive men? To Jan, to Mike, even, in a way to Dirk, who had had to make do with my company at Scheveningen when he would have preferred Sally's, I was merely a stand-in for the woman they desired and on whom they had set their sights.

Mike's voice brought both Jan and me from our sad reveries.

"I think it is time we returned to Apelward," he said. "Mr. and Mrs. Starke are expecting us at mid-day for a farewell lunch, and it would be rude to keep them waiting, after all their kindness to us."

138

# Chapter 11

To my surprise, when we returned to the Starkes' farmhouse, Dirk van der Woude was there, standing chatting to Anna's parents in the pleasant living room overlooking the garden.

Sally was as taken aback at seeing him as I was, and also, as I deduced from the flush which crept into her cheeks, more than a shade embarrassed.

She was aware that she had encouraged his attentions the day we had first met him, and had continued to flirt lightly with him at Scheveningen, although she was teasing him with her interest in Mike, and accordingly he had found an excuse to come to Apelward to continue the game, in which case he must be more than mildly interested in her to make the long journey.

"What are you doing here?" she greeted him sharply. "I didn't know you were a friend of Mr. and Mrs. Starke."

"Aren't you pleased to see me, Sally?" he replied, with a teasing twinkle in his eyes.

Sally's flush deepened, and for the first time since I had known her she seemed at loss for words.

Mrs. Starke, noting Sally's uncomfortable reaction, and no doubt guessing at the reason for it from the way Dirk was moving closer to her, eyed him as if he was an unwanted intruder and came to her rescue.

"Mr. van der Woude has come here to have a word with Janey about some business matter which has cropped up in The Hague." She turned to me with a smile. "I hope it is nothing serious."

Sally's jaw slacked in astonishment at her words, but she was no more astonished than I was.

"What business?" I scowled at Dirk.

"I shall tell you what it is about in private," he said briskly. "Will you excuse us, please?" He looked at Mr. and Mrs. Starke, who both nodded.

Van der Woude took me by the arm with a friendliness in the gesture which did not please Jan Stuyvesant. He made to follow us through the french window into the garden, as if he was as suspicious about the reason for Dirk's visit as I was, but his uncle put out a detaining hand, muttered some words in his ear, words which I could only faintly distinguish, about van der Woude being here on official business. These words did not make sense to me, and I decided I must have misinterpreted the Dutch.

Once in the garden, I stopped short and pulled my arm from Dirk's now not-so-friendly grasp.

"Tell me," I said sharply. "What is all this about? What is your real reason for coming to Apelward? You don't fool me for a moment with this excuse of business."

"It isn't an excuse." He shook his head. "But let's get a little further from the house before I explain."

Once again he took my arm, and together we strolled past the farm and the shrubbery of lilac bushes and on along the tow path, more like friends or lovers than two people about to engage on a business conversation.

He remained silent for so long, without giving his explanations, that I became annoyed.

"Dirk, if this is some silly ploy of yours," I muttered angrily, "some childish way of making Sally jealous, I don't think it's clever or amusing. If it isn't a game, will you kindly explain why you are here as soon as possible? I don't want to keep lunch waiting!"

Van der Woude's eyes narrowed.

"I don't understand your reference to Sally," he retorted, "unless you are being clever and trying to cloud the issue.

"I wonder just how clever you are, Janey," he continued in a harsh voice, "and just how surprised you will pretend to be when I tell you that I came here to tell you that the police in

141

The Hague wish to interview you about a certain very serious matter!"

I gaped at him in utter surprise.

"Now I know you are amusing yourself at my expense!" I said explosively. "Couldn't you think up some more plausible reason for coming here?"

"I am stating a fact, not making up an excuse to come here, as you pretend to think," he replied. "The police in The Hague are very anxious to find you and ask you a few questions."

I laughed without amusement.

"Don't be silly! Why should the police be interested in me? Unless—" I frowned, stopping short.

"Yes?" he rapped out.

"Is it about the lad who fell from the fire escape?" I asked. "Did you tell them I had noticed him in the lounge in the evening? Do they want me to identify him, or something?"

"He has been identified," van der Woude replied, his eyes searching my face. "His name is Hans Vogel."

"If they know who he is, why do the police want to see me especially? Plenty of other people must have seen him in the Collenius. What about the group of young people he was with?"

"They had never set eyes on him before he sat down at the table beside them. He came in alone, and they thought he was waiting for someone."

"Still, they would have seen more of him than I did, so why the police interest in me?"

"Because," van der Woude's lips tightened in a grim line, "they think you knew him, or he knew you, and had come to the Collenius to meet you!"

He pulled me to a standstill as he uttered the last words, moving in front of me as he did so, so that we were facing each other. His gaze was fixed, staring into my eyes, as if he was trying to read my mind.

I was so taken aback at what he had said that I couldn't find words to reply. I stood there, staring at him, my mouth drooping with shock, my mind numbed with incredulity at his accusation.

"Janey!" He spoke my name softly, almost sadly. "Listen to me, please. If you have been up to something silly, if you have been trying to oblige a friend by, say—" He stopped, bit his lip, and looked at me with frowning concentration before he continued slowly.—"By getting hold of a parcel of some kind to smuggle back to England for them, please, please tell me! I might be able to help you."

I took a deep breath and shook my head.

"One of us," I murmured, "one of us is stark, raving mad, and it isn't me! I haven't the faintest idea what you are talking about!"

Van der Woude continued to gaze at me with a thoughtful expression, and I stared back at him, my eyes unwavering.

I was very aware of the mid-day sun on my

143

head; of the soft breeze which riffled through the grass at the edge of the canal and rustled through the drooping willow leaves which the calm water reflected back. I was conscious of the murmur of the bees in the lilac trees which shaded the south wall of the farmhouse, and the lapping of wavelets against the hull of the dinghy moored under the trees. I heard the faint sound of voices and laughter which drifted through the open window of the living room; I noticed, in fact, all the pleasant realities around me, because my mind wanted to be aware of them, to linger on them, to keep at bay the shocking idea that Dirk van der Woude, the man I found so beguiling and attractive, considered me capable of being involved in some kind of criminal venture.

It was Dirk who broke the silence between us, and his voice was chill.

"I am talking about a youngster of eighteen who is dead." He eyed me coldly. "Dead because he was a drug addict. Dead because he was desperate to get more drugs to satisfy his craving. Dead because he thought he knew where he could get some!

"Yes, Miss Mathieson." There wasn't a whit of friendliness now in van der Woude's voice. "Hans Vogel is dead, because in trying to break into your bedroom in the Collenius to get hold of the packet he had been unable to obtain when his reckless attempt to snatch away your handbag in the Lange Voorhout failed, he slipped on the rain-slimed rungs of the fire escape when attempting to swing across to your balcony, and fell head-first on to the concrete patio below!"

I didn't believe him. I didn't want to believe him.

"You're making this up!" I protested. "And it isn't funny! It isn't funny at all!" I shivered as I spoke.

"No, it isn't funny, is it?" His eyes bored into mine. "But you know I am not making up the story, don't you? You know what young Vogel was after!" he accused me.

I felt cold to the core. So cold that in spite of the heat of the sun on my shoulders, I shivered.

So graphic had been van der Woude's description of the accident that in my mind's eye I could see the sickly-faced lad in the blue polo-neck shirt go scrambling up the fire escape, regardless of the blustering wind and the torrential rain, all his senses dulled to everything but his awful craving to get at the drug which would give him momentary release from his anguish, a drug he appeared to think I had in my possession.

I could visualize his insane attempt to bridge the gap between fire escape and balcony; imagine his fear as he felt his foothold slip, felt his grasp sliding away. I almost relived his panic when he found he could find no fresh foothold and that he hadn't the strength in his fingers to cling to the railing, and I could almost hear his scream as his hands slithered uselessly down the railing and he went plunging downward.

Involuntarily my hand went to my mouth to stifle my own cry of shock.

Van der Woude sneered at the gesture.

"So you do have some feelings?"

I stared at him, wide-eyed. The coldness of horror gave way to a hot flush of anger as the full realization of what I was being accused of by the man facing me dawned on me.

I rounded on him fiercely.

"What kind of woman do you think I am, van der Woude?" I grated, calling him by his surname to show my contempt of him. "Do you honestly think I had something to do with that wretched boy's death? Do I look to you the kind of person who would have truck with drug traffickers?" I gazed at him wrathfully.

"Let me tell you," I continued, "I despise, I loathe, the people who engage in this trade. As a nurse, during training I saw, unfortunately far too often, the results of drug addiction. I have seen the degradation, the heartache, the misery, the appalling waste of young lives it causes.

"I have worked with addicts; worked in wards to which they are brought, and to which young people should be taken so that they can learn in time the truth about the so-called euphoria these drugs bring!

"Yes!" I ranted on, my voice shrill with protest. "I wish every rotten man and woman who grows fat and opulent on the vile trade they foster could be made to pay for the human misery for which they are responsible."

146

I stopped for breath, and still glaring at him, continued.

"And to think that you, that you could accuse me of being a part of such an organization, a part of such—of such—filth! I am outraged! Outraged! And to think I imagined I liked you!"

With that, I turned my back to him and stormed off back to the farmhouse, although I was so shaky with nerves and anger my legs felt they would collapse under me.

Dirk hurried after me and caught up with me as I reached the clump of lilacs.

"Janey!" he cried.

Once again he pulled me to a standstill.

"Listen to me. I had to say what I said! I was stating the police case; what they are assuming from the affair. They don't know you as a person as I do. They make their deductions impersonally, from the facts they are presented with!"

"Facts! What facts? How can I be implicated?"

"To begin with, the young man who made such an open and reckless attempt to relieve you of your handbag in the Lange Voorhout was the same young man who made an equally reckless and unsuccessful attempt to get into your bedroom that same night, and the police think that is too much of a coincidence to swallow!"

"How do the police know that it was the same man?" I pooh-poohed the idea. "You said yourself that my description of the bag snatcher fitted scores of young people who roam the city! And in any case, the boy in the hotel was dressed differently. He was wearing a blue polo

147

neck, not a leather jerkin, and he had on sun glasses, the other one didn't . . ." My voice tailed off.

I remembered the eyes of the bag snatcher, the only feature of him which had been visible, and there had been that peculiar look in them which should have told me, with my experience, that he took drugs.

Dirk explained.

"The cloakroom attendant recognized the description of the dead man. He said he had handed over a leather jerkin to his keeping earlier in the evening. The jerkin hadn't been claimed by mid-day, and when the police examined it, they found a balaclava stuffed into a pocket, and further evidence that it belonged to the victim."

"Even so, how did he know to come to the Collenius to look for me, if it was me he was looking for?"

Dirk considered me carefully.

"Don't you remember, Janey? You told Sally and me you were sure you saw your bag snatcher loitering in a shop doorway as we entered Molen Straat. We disagreed with you, but it would seem you were right, and Vogel was deliberately keeping a watch on you, to find out where you were staying."

"But why did he choose me of all people?" I cried. "I had only been in The Hague for twenty-four hours! He couldn't possibly have seen me before, unless—" I paused. "Yes, that will be the reason." I nodded to myself. "He obviously mistook me for someone else!"

Van der Woude eyed me gravely.

"That must be the answer. Yes! Of course it is the answer!" He gave me a reassuring smile. "Vogel thought you were someone else. When you make your statement to the police, they will realize this too!" His smile grew, as if he was delighted at this, to me, obvious solution. "The sooner you go to them and talk to them, the sooner they will be able to concentrate on running the real contact to ground! "Come!" He took my arm, and was about to walk forward to the house, but I held him back.

"There is one thing which still puzzles me," I challenged him. "Why didn't the police come to Apelward themselves, to see me? Where do you fit into all this?"

Dirk hesitated before replying.

"As a matter of fact," he said slowly, "they don't know where you are. Neither you nor Sally mentioned to the hotel management that you would be away overnight. No one knew where you had gone off to—and I'm afraid this added to their suspicions!"

"But you knew!" I pointed out, "So why didn't you tell them?"

"Yes," he agreed, "I knew where you had gone to yesterday, and I suspected you might be staying the night here, having," he smiled, "been a guest myself at Dutch weddings in the past. The wedding was the reason I didn't want officials to come out here and upset things. The Starkes are influential people in this area, and it would have been a difficult situation for them, as well as for you."

I was still puzzled.

"But how did you know the police were so eager to make contact with me, and why didn't you let things be until I returned to The Hague? You knew I would be back!"

"I have a number of friends in The Hague, Janey. The Commissaird of police is one of them. I knew what was going on from a conversation, and I decided it would be for the best all around if I decided to come to Apelward and bring you back to The Hague myself.

"In the first place, it would save the Starkes embarrassment, for they certainly would not like to have police cars on their doorstep at this particular time. In the second place—" he paused.

"Yes?" I queried.

There was a curious expression in van der Woude's eyes as he replied.

"In the second place, Janey, a man likes to be proved right in his judgment, although he knows that his judgment can sometimes be wrong, because friendship blinds him to the faults of those he likes."

He gave a shamefaced grin.

"I wanted to be certain I was right about you, Janey, before I threw you to the wolves, so to speak. I am sorry, very sorry, my dear, that I should have doubted you as I did, even if it was only for a moment. But then," he sighed, "in my business we are prone to doubt. Will you forgive me, Janey?"

"I'll try." I forced a smile, but deep inside I still felt sad that this man I liked so much should have suspected me, even if only for a brief space of time, of being involved with the distribution of drugs.

with about forty-odd stairs in my ... I gave Sally and Klaus ... night hug to ...

*Chapter 12*

I explained to the Starkes that the police in The Hague thought that I might be able to help them in their inquiries in connection with an accident at the hotel, and Dirk had come to drive me back to the city.

Dirk took it from there, and explained further that there was nothing to worry about. I was not personally involved. It was merely a question of confirming certain facts. Before leaving for my brother's wedding, I had intimated that I was willing to help in any way, and now a matter had arisen which I might be able to clarify.

As a friend, he had decided to come and fetch me in person, rather than start up any wild rumors in the village by letting me be sent for in an official car.

"Is it about the boy who fell from the fire escape?" asked Sally.

I nodded. "Yes."

She pursed her lips and said in warning, "For goodness sake don't mention that Tim might have seen the lad too, or he might be dragged back from his honeymoon! He would never forgive you if that happened!"

The Starkes looked so upset at this possibility that I hastened to put their minds at ease.

"I am quite sure Tim didn't notice him, and I certainly have no intention of making any mention of him," I said firmly.

"Janey, if there is any trouble, or if the police try to bully you in any way, let me know!" put in Jan Stuyvesant aggressively. "I know the head men in the force, both in The Hague and in Amsterdam, so if you have anything to complain about, I'll have something to say to them!"

Van der Woude scowled at his words, but he said nothing.

"At least you will have something to eat before you leave," Mrs Starke insisted. "You will join us for lunch, won't you, Mr. van der Woude?"

I had little appetite for food. I was unhappy about the situation in which I found myself. It shocked me that the police in The Hague suspected me of being involved in dope smuggling, and innocent though I was, I felt as if I was guilty of some misdemeanor merely because of their unwarranted suspicions.

Mike and Sally decided to leave for The Hague immediately after lunch as well.

Jan came out to see me off in Dirk's car. He took my hand in his powerful grip and told me not to worry about anything.

"If you have any problems, my dear, you just let me know and I'll see what I can do.

"In any event, Janey," he looked down at me, "I shall see you for lunch on Tuesday. You hadn't forgotten our date, had you?"

"Of course not!" I smiled back at him. His genuine concern for me was heartening, and I added warmly, "I am looking forward to it, Jan."

Mike and Sally drove off first, and Dirk and I followed. Mike drove at speed and soon moved out of our range of vision, for Dirk, in spite of the urgency he had stressed, was not prepared to use the road like a race track.

It was another sunlit afternoon, but today I could not enjoy the return journey to The Hague as I had enjoyed the drive to Apelward. For one thing, the roads were busy with Sunday traffic, which took the edge off the remembered tranquility of the outward journey, and for another, my own thoughts were as chaotic and erratic as the pattern of the Sunday afternoon motorists.

Dirk stole a glance at my troubled face as I sat stolidly beside him, my hands on my lap, my fingers twining and intertwining nervously with each other.

"Janey, everything is going to be all right," he conforted me. "You are innocent of any criminal activity so you have nothing to worry about. The police will soon realize, once they question you, that your involvement in the case was purely accidental and that they will have to look elsewhere for Vogel's supplier."

He took a hand off the steering wheel and grasped my restless fingers in his warm clasp, giving them a reassuring squeeze.

"If you like, I shall sit in with you on the inquisition!" he proposed.

I gave him a grateful look.

"It would be nice to have a friend at court, so to speak!" I said hopefully. "But I don't expect the police would let you do that, would they? Not when it's an official interview."

"I'll tell them I'm your lawyer!" He grinned. "They would accept me then!"

"Dirk! No. You would get into trouble. I won't have that," I said firmly. "Thanks all the same. It was a kind thought."

"But I am a lawyer, among other things," he stated. "I would be telling the truth!"

"Oh!" I stared at him with surprise. "I didn't know that. You didn't tell me what your occupation was."

"You never asked." He grinned. "In any case," he added in a more serious tone, "I don't like telling people what my profession is."

"I can understand that." I smiled. "If you did, people would keep asking you for free advice. I know that my uncle, who is a doctor, never lets on that he is in the medical profession when he is on holiday; otherwise he would find his time taken up listening to tales of people's ailments, and he would be expected to give a diagnosis or suggest a remedy on the spot. It would be like being back home in his surgery, instead of getting away from it all!"

We had come to the Ijsslmeer dyke, but although I still experienced a twinge of uneasiness as we drove along it, out of sight of land and with the water lapping on either side, today, because of the number of cars on the road, it did not seem such a desolate and eerie drive as it had the first time I had crossed it. Moreover, Dirk kept up a cheerful flow of conversation which distracted my attention from the scene, and I wasn't the forgotten, odd woman out I had been with Mike and Sally.

Dirk asked me how the wedding had gone and if I had enjoyed the Dutch-style celebrations.

"It was marvelous!" I beamed in recollection. "But I don't know where the guests got all their stamina, to carry on the way they did throughout the day and into the night! As a matter of fact, after the wedding breakfast and before the afternoon reception, Sally and I discreetly retired to the room the Starkes had booked for us in a local hotel, to have a short rest so that we would be fit for the rest of the fray!"

"Who is the blond giant who is taking you to lunch on Tuesday?" Dirk dropped the question casually.

"Jan Stuyvesant," I replied. "Didn't the Starkes introduce you to him? He is a cousin of Anna, their daughter—Tim's bride."

"It is obvious he finds you very attractive."

I blushed.

"I think the main attraction is that I am someone on whom he can practice his English!" I said with a deprecatory shrug. "Also the fact

156

that he was big Jan and I was little Janey appealed to his sense of humor."

"I think there is more to it than that," persisted Dirk. "He looked at you in a special sort of way. Possibly it is the attraction of opposites." He gave me a sideways glance. "You are so slim and petite and he is such a giant of a man. Moreover, Janey, you have a very appealing way with you. It brings out the protective nature in a man!"

"Don't be silly!" I protested. "Everyone at the wedding appeared to have a partner, so Jan took pity on me, and I was grateful. After all," I pointed out, "a girl does need someone to dance with at a wedding!"

We lapsed into silence for a time as we drove through Amsterdam, and on the last stages of the drive, past the tulip fields and along the tree-lined motorway which led to The Hague, our conversation was desultory and spasmodic.

I found myself thinking more and more about the interview which lay ahead of me, and I couldn't concentrate on what Dirk was saying to me. Although I kept telling myself there was nothing for me to worry about, although I knew that there should be nothing for me to worry about, what if the police continued to think otherwise? What if they continued to suspect me because Vogel had mistaken me for someone else? What would happen then?

I fidgeted uneasily in my seat, and although my eyes were set in a fixed stare out of the side window, I saw nothing of the countryside which flashed past; nothing of the parklands and the handsome houses of wealthy suburbanites set in equally handsome gardens, well back from the noise and bustle of the motorway.

"Of course they are bound to realize that Vogel mistook me for someone else."

I spoke the words aloud to give me more assurance.

Dirk turned a startled stare in my direction.

"What was that you said?"

"I said the police are bound to realize that Vogel took me for someone else. It happens all the time to me. I seem to be that kind of person."

"What do you mean?" frowned Dirk.

"I have quite often been mistaken for someone else, but particularly so these past few days. Miss Average Woman, that's me! Someone fated never to be loved for myself!" I gave a half-hysterical giggle.

"Take Mike, now. I remind Mike of his sister, who is small and slim and fair-haired, so he treats me like a sister. I remind Jan Stuyvesant of the girl he left behind in Vermont, the girl he had hoped to marry, so he dances with me and romances with me, pretending that I am she! You—"

"Yes, what about me?" He cocked his head to one side interrogatively. "Of whom do you think you remind me?"

"I don't think!" I retorted. "I know! You told me yourself!"

He looked puzzled. "I think you must be mixing me up with someone else."

"No. You told me that I reminded you of the rag doll I liked in the market. The one you asked the stallholder to put aside for me, but which I didn't get, after all!" I sighed.

"And talking of rag dolls," I went on with a sudden frown, "I suppose it was mere coincidence that Hans Vogel wasn't the only one who was curious to have a look at my possessions. There was that chambermaid at the Collenius, remember I mentioned her to you? I was annoyed at the way she ripped the seam of my rag doll when she went through my things."

"You know, I had forgotten about that!" Dirk bit his lower lip with vexation. "That was very stupid of me! I wonder—"

"What do you wonder?" I looked at him anxiously, but he ignored my question and fixed his eyes steadfastly on the road ahead, as if he had something on his mind and wanted to think about it without interruption.

A mile slipped silently past, and now we were in The Hague and slowing down to find a parking place near the police station.

I felt sick with nerves; I did not think my legs would be firm enough to carry me along the road to the entrance.

"It's all right, Janey." Dirk took me by the arm. "Remember, I am going to substitute for Jan and play the part of your protective heman," he joked. "I'll make sure that no one tries to bully you!"

Although, in spite of what he had said, I had been doubtful that van der Woude would be allowed to stay with me throughout the inverview, I was delighted when no objection was made to his staying with me while the Commissair put his questions.

All in all, the interview was not as nerve-racking as I had imagined it might be. There was a relaxed atmosphere about the proceedings, and Commissair Markheim seemed determined to put me at my ease.

After a few formal questions about myself, I was asked why I had come to Holland and why I had chosen to stay at the Collenius. I was asked for the names of anyone I knew who was a Dutch resident, and the officer's eyebrows were raised more than a fraction when I gave the names of my brother's father and mother-in-law, and Jan Stuyvesant of Leeuwarden.

I was now asked to give an account of my actions from the moment of my arrival at Schiphol airport, until the morning following Vogel's death.

Dirk van der Woude was able to confirm much of what I told the police, and they seemed pleased to accept my straightforward narrative. One of the points I made, about how my room had been searched by the chambermaid, interested them particularly, which surprised me, for to me it had seemed unimportant and I would not have mentioned it if Dirk hadn't prompted me to do so.

When I had finished my recital there was a

prolonged silence, and the Commissair glanced at his notes and made a few additions.

I hoped the interview was over, but it appeared Markheim still had a few more questions to ask me.

"Miss Mathieson, tell me. At any time before or immediately after your arrival in Holland, did anyone give you a parcel to look after for them?"

This was the same question which Dirk had earlier asked me, and as I had done on that occasion, I shook my head and answered in the negative.

"Could anyone have slipped a parcel into your handbag by error when you were shopping at the market in the Lange Voorhout, for example?"

I shook my head again, lifted my handbag from my knees and dumped it on the desk in front of him.

"Not without a certain amount of difficulty, as you will deduce," I remarked dryly. "When I tell you that on that particular day I had a large rag doll stuffed on top of this lot, you will appreciate that it would have been well nigh impossible!"

For the first time since I had met him, Markheim smiled a smile of genuine amusement.

"I see what you mean, Miss Mathieson."

He sat back in his chair and tapped the desk with his pen as he said, with a note of exasperation in his voice, "There doesn't seem to be much more that you can tell us, is there? It would appear that for some reason which we shall probably never learn, Vogel mistook you for someone else.".

He sighed. "We seemed to have such a good lead this time! Now we shall have to go back to square one. You can't think of any more questions to put to Miss Mathieson which might help us?" He looked hopefully at the faces of the other two men who were in the room, and I could not understand why his glance should linger in Dirk's direction.

"If you have no more questions to put to my friend," interposed Dirk swiftly, "there is no point in keeping her here any longer, is there?"

Markheim shook his head, thanked me for the help I had given, and stood up to shake hands with me.

"It was very good of you to spare time from your holiday to come and help us, Miss Mathieson," he remarked suavely as he escorted me to the door.

I tried not to smile, for I knew it had not been a question of my coming to the police station of my own free will. If Dirk hadn't come for me and made it seem that my arrival had been voluntary, I had no doubt I would have been sent for, without the choice of refusal.

"Thank goodness that's over!" I breathed with relief as we left the building. "Let's get back to the Collenius. Sally and Mike will be waiting for us there and wondering what has been going on. We can set their minds at ease over a long, ice-cold drink!"

Dirk stopped and looked at me, and I sensed

he was going to refuse the suggestion. I could hardly blame him. He had already done a great deal to help me today, what with his long drive to Apelward and back, and the way he had helped me during my session with the police. By this time he was no doubt tired of the sight of me.

"I'm sorry!" I sighed. "I was being very selfish, asking you to waste more time over my affairs." I forced a smile. "You must be tired of playing father protector to me today, and doubtless you have other plans for the evening. If you tell me the quickest way to walk back to the Collenius from here, I shall find my own way there."

"Don't be silly, Janey!" he replied briskly. "I have every intention of taking you back to your hotel, but first I have to make a phone call. While I do that, you can go to the car and wait for me there. I'll give you the keys."

"But—"

"No buts, sweetheart," he said with a smile. "I like your suggestion of a long, cool drink. I might even let you pay for it, as part of my legal fee," he joked. "Oh, and by the way," he hastened to add, "I wouldn't say too much about your interview to Sally and Mike. Merely mention that the police were checking to make sure that the boy in the lounge and the boy who died were one and the same. For that matter you could say they believe he mistook you for someone else and was trying to get in your window, but I'd leave it at that."

"Legal advice from my lawyer, I take it?" I smiled at him.

"Sound advice, Janey, from someone with your interests very much at heart!"

He looked down at me as he was speaking, and for a moment we gazed directly into one another's eyes before I looked quickly away.

When Dirk spoke to me in such a gentle tone, when he uttered my name as if he enjoyed saying it, when he looked at me with his intensely blue eyes, I felt my breath catch in my throat, my pulsebeat race, and a betraying flush of emotion creep into my cheeks.

In short, I felt like a schoolgirl in the presence of her pin-up idol. I also felt a fool because I seemed to have no control over my emotions, and I was so afraid that Dirk might realize how I was feeling that I felt I had to say something to cover my confusion.

"I hope you don't expect another drink for the extra advice!"

I wondered at the calm tone of my voice as I forced the joking words.

"Let us say, in your case, I give the extra advice for love."

"Love as in tennis?" I quipped flippantly.

"Of course!" he said gruffly. "Here are the keys." He dropped them into the palm of my hand. "Off you go to the car. I shall only be gone a few minutes."

I walked away from him, clutching the keys tightly in my palm, feeling on them the lingering warmth of Dirk's hand. I wished as I turned the corner, that it was his hand in mine I could feel; wished that I had met Dirk van der Woude in other circumstances; wished that he wouldn't merely think of me as a nusiance of a girl who had got into difficulties in a foreign land, and whom, because of his kindly and quixotic nature, he felt bound to help.

## Chapter 13

When we arrived at the Collenius, I wasn't at all pleased to find Oliver Saunders, Natasha Berg and their two friends seated at the same table as Mike and Sally, enjoying a light-hearted conversation as they sipped ice-chilled Martinis.

I sensed, from the way Dirk's fingers tightened on my arm as he ushered me through the doorway, that he felt the same as I did.

"Hey, Janey!" Saunders greeted me. "What is this I hear about you being femme fatale and luring some poor boy to his death?"

Before I could answer, Sally said swiftly, "There are all sorts of rumors floating around the hotel, but the most popular one is that the dead boy was an old flame of yours."

"That's rubbish! I'd like to know who starts such stupid talk."

"I got the story from the barman!" leered Saunders. "He said he overheard a couple of policemen talking, and they were saying that the boy had been following you around all day, and was trying to steal from you!"

"And I was saying you didn't have anything to steal that was worth the trouble he had gone to," murmured Sally.

"It is true though, isn't it," put in Natasha, "that the police sent for you?" There was malice in her voice. "What have you been up to?"

"Nothing!" I retorted. "I told them it was obviously a case of mistaken identity. They seemed satisfied with that."

Saunders looked peeved. "I was hoping I might be able to come to your aid. It would have been good publicity for us if a TV detective solved the mystery before the official."

"We might still get some publicity from it," suggested Frankie Donaldson, the fourth member of the Natasha circle, a man I disliked for no good reason except that he made me feel ill at ease.

Looking at him as he spoke, I tried to hide my distaste, not only for him but for his companions and their craze for publicity.

I had been a fool to accept Saunders' invitation to go with him to see over the studios at Bussum on Wednesday, but I had been too stubborn to admit my mistake until now. It was small wonder that Sally, who had known him better than I did, had been annoyed with me for saying yes to him.

"Who did the boy think you were?" Saunders ogled me, while Dirk, his lips tight with annoyance, went over to the bar to get me the long

167

drink of ice-cold orange I had asked him to bring me.

"Or maybe," he joked, "it wasn't you he was after. Perhaps it was that gorgeous doll you bought in the market and showed off to us. The one with the tantalizing red apple on her bib. I rather fancied her myself."

"Stop being frivolous, Oliver," snapped Natasha.

"I wasn't being frivolous," he sneered at her. "I prefer baby dolls to women of the world. They aren't so shop-soiled and bored with life, and," his glance shifted from Natasha's beautifully madeup mask of a face to my glowing skin, "they stand the test of age better. Don't you agree, Frankie?"

Natasha's pupils narrowed into pinpoints of fury. I didn't like her but I felt that Saunders had gone over the score in needling her the way he was doing. However, Natasha was able to give as good as she got.

"The poor boy who died may have been a drug addict, Oliver, but I am sure he wasn't a pervert who liked to take dolls to bed with him!"

Having got his own jibe in, Saunders ignored her response and reverted his attention to me, asking me if perhaps there had been something else I had bought at the market which Vogel had been after.

"I saw nothing else which appealed to me, except for your chessboards." I smiled at Dirk.

"You couldn't have been looking very carefully," said Sanders. "What do you think of my ring? I got it for next to nothing!"

He held out his hand to display a dress ring on his little finger. To me it was an ugly ring. It was too broad, too ornate, with what I took to be the phoenix rising from the contorted strands of silver which represented flames. Yet my gaze continued to rest on his hand, with its wrinkled skin and square, stubby little fingers, and on the design of the ring, which made me think of flames and burns, and with a suddenness which made me speak out abruptly, a flash of memory came to mind.

"I knew I had seen him before!" I gasped.

Oliver Saunders withdrew his hand with an abrupt gesture, and the circle of faces around the table riveted their attention on me.

"Who was it you saw before?" asked Dirk quietly.

"The man in the green Audi outside the Park Hotel in Apelward!"

"What man was this?" he frowned.

"The man with the scarred hands. Hands which had been scarred by burning! Oliver's phoenix triggered off a memory which has been at the back of my mind!"

"Slowly, my dear!" pleaded Dirk. "Who was he? Where did you first see him?"

"The first time, he was sitting over there," I nodded toward a table on the perimeter of the lounge, between the cocktail bar and the corridor leading to the Vermeer Room. "I felt even then that he was watching me covertly."

"Another old man with an eye for young girls?" sneered Nastasha.

I ignored her.

"Hans Vogel, the lad who fell from the fire escape, was seated at the table right next to him. They could have been together!"

"So what?" Saunders looked puzzled.

"I don't know," I said thoughtfully. "But the next time I saw that man with the scarred hand, he was outside the Park Hotel in Apelward where Sally and I were staying last night. He was staring around as if he was looking for someone, and in fact," I looked at Mike, "he had a good look at your car as if he was checking up on it!"

"That's odd," scowled Mike. "It was a green Audi which was following us yesterday, from Amsterdam and along the Ijsslmeer dyke, until I lost it with a burst of speed, remember?"

Sally and I nodded as Mike added, "Come to think of it, a green Audi passed us outside The Hague station, and kept ahead of us all the way to Amsterdam."

"Are you certain it was the same man you saw?" demanded Dirk.

"Positive! Our bedroom in the Park was on the first floor, with a balcony overlooking the street. The Audi was parked almost directly below, under the chestnut trees. I could see the man, but I doubt if he was aware of my presence. I kept watching him, because his movements intrigued me. Then, when he put out his hand to open the car door, I noticed the

170

scarring. I knew at the time it reminded me of someone, as did the squat figure and the curling gray hair, but I couldn't think who."

"You didn't say anything to me about this!" said Sally. "If you thought there was something familiar about the man, why didn't you tell me?"

"Because," I reminded her dryly, "the last time I thought I recognized someone, you and Dirk," I turned to van der Woude accusingly, "made fun of me, and you would have made fun of me again, wouldn't you?"

She bit her lip.

"Is that why you were looking so worried when you came in from the balcony?" she demanded. "I thought—" she stopped short, and a slow blush crimsoned her cheeks as she remembered the conversation which had followed on that occasion.

"This would make a great plot for your next film, Oliver!" said Frankie with enthusiasm. "The Man in the Green Audi! How is that for a title?"

Sally interrupted him with a faintly hysterical note in her voice.

"Janey!" Her overloud tone attracted the attention of the people at the next table and of the passing waiter who stopped, thinking she had been trying to attract his attention, but she waved him away.

"Remember I accused you of rummaging through my case in the Park this morning? And you said," she gulped nervously, "you said your

171

things had been tampered with as well, and we blamed the chambermaid! You don't think it could have been this man, do you? I mean, how could he get in to our room?

"Oh!" Her hand went to her mouth to tone down her startled gasp. "Your nightmare! Maybe you did see someone on the balcony!"

"That's enough," said Dirk sharply. "The pair of you have had too much excitement yesterday and today, and now you are beginning to let your imaginations run away with you!

"Come along, Sally, Janey, drink up!" he ordered in a peremptory tone, glancing at his watch. "It's four o'clock. I have to leave soon, and I still have to see the snapshots you promised to show me, and which you left in the room."

Natasha was reluctant to lose our company. "It's only five to," she pointed out, but taking Dirk's words as a signal that it was not wise of us to say any more about our suspicions in public, we ignored her and stood up to go.

Before we left, Oliver wanted to confirm the arrangements for Wednesday.

I hesitated. "Could we leave it, meantime?" I asked. "Tomrrow we are going to Keukenhof, and on Tuesday I have a date with a family friend."

Dirk's eyebrows shot up at this description of Jan Stuyvesant, but he made no snide remark.

"That still leaves Wednesday free," persisted Oliver.

"I want to visit the Mauritshuis sometime. It is a must for me."

"You can't turn me down in favor of a few cracked old paintings," Saunders leered at me. "And you promised—"

"I shall let you know later," I said firmly. "I hadn't expected today to be taken up with police interviews, and this has left me very little time to see all the places I am keen to see."

"That is one bet I win!" Natasha smiled with satisfaction. "Oliver, I told you she would find an excuse to opt out!"

"She hasn't opted out yet!" Saunders refused to concede. "We'll wait until Wednesday before we settle!"

"Don't be mean, Oliver," piped Frankie. "It will be good for Natasha's morale to win a bet for a change!"

We left them arguing, and crossed to the lift.

"That's my girl!" Dirk approved as we were whisked to the second floor. "I'm glad you have come to your senses. Saunders is not the kind of man a girl like you should tangle with. He should be left to the Natashas of this world."

The lift stopped and we got out and went to Sally's room. She unlocked the door, turning to me as she did so to tell me that she had collected my case, as well as her own, from the hotel in Apelward on her way back to The Hague.

"Thanks, Sally! I had forgotten my case was still at the hotel!"

"May I have a look at it?" demanded Dirk, following us into the room.

"What for?" I looked at him.

"For the same reason I broke up the party in the lounge to come up here," he replied crisply. "I want to ask a few more questions about the man in the Audi, and this nightmare you had."

"You are acting like a policeman!" I said angrily. "I have had enough of them for one day!"

"I'm afraid you will have to put up with them for a little longer," he retorted. "Something very odd is going on, and you seem to be in the center of it. We have to find out what it is."

"We?" I said slowly.

"Yes, we. I didn't want to have to tell you, but the fact is, I am a police officer, special branch, working with the Commissair here on a narcotics inquiry involving The Hague—London connection."

"That explains a few things," commented Mike. "I was wondering about you, after you came to Apelward and took Janey away to see the Commissair."

"You should have told us about yourself before now," Sally reproved him.

"I didn't want it generally known." Dirk looked at me as he spoke, but I remained silent and tried to hide the hurt I felt on discovering that his interest in me was official and not personal.

"I hope you will forgive me, Janey, but I have already searched through your belongings in the hotel here, as I searched your handbag at Scheveningen, when I knocked it from your hand 'accidentally' "

174

He crossed to the telephone.

"Before I go any further, I must tell Markheim about your man with the scars on his hands. He may know something about him."

While he talked to his colleague, Sally and Mike stood holding hands and whispering together. I crossed to the window and stared unseeing over the lilacs and the rooftops.

"That's that!" Dirk replaced the receiver after his conversation with headquarters. "Now, please, may I examine your case?"

"Do you think Saunders may have had a point about it being the doll the men are after?" suggested Mike. "There could be something stuffed inside it."

"We examined the doll."

"Yes," Sally blurted out the words, "but you didn't examine the dragon, and they wouldn't have known where to look for it!" She stared at him, round-eyed.

"What are you talking about?" he demanded.

"Janey bought a dragon for me," she called over her shoulder as she went hurrying to the bathroom. She came back bearing the half-polished ornament. "Do you think this is what all the fuss has been about?"

Dirk looked at the ugly ornament and weighed it in his hand.

"I doubt if it could contain what we are looking for, and it seems pretty solid." He eyed it critically, and his fingers felt over the surface. "It has been a bit bashed about, hasn't it." He touched the indentation. "But wait a minute!"

175

He held the dragon up for a closer scrutiny. "This piece looks as if it has been recently welded to the original. Didn't you notice?"

"You wouldn't have noticed very much the way it was when I bought it," I remarked. "It was embedded with grime and dried-up polish!"

"So?" Dirk's expression grew thoughtful.

"Sally," he appealed to my friend. "Would you mind if I broke open your ornament?"

She hesitated. "If you think it would solve anything, no."

"In that case, thanks!" He pocketed the creature. "Wait here until I get in touch with you!" He moved to the door. "I think we shall perform the operation in the privacy of police headquarters, with Markheim as my chief assistant."

Half an hour later his call came through, and I took it.

"Janey." He recognized my voice. "We want you to meet us at the Café Marietta at the corner of the alley which joins Nordeinde." He sounded cheerful. "There is a private room there, where we can talk things over without being overheard or having the meeting connected with police business.

"We shall even stand you your coffees at public expense." I could picture the twinkle in his eyes as he spoke. "You have put us on to something very interesting!"

"Don't keep us in suspense," I pleaded. "You found something, didn't you?"

"We found diamonds!" he announced. "A small fortune in uncut diamonds!"

176

*Chapter 14*

The Café Marietta was a clever choice of meeting place for the formal interview we had with Commissair Markheim. I found the atmosphere less inhibiting than the atmosphere of the police station, and this made it easier for me to talk about how the dragon came to be purchased by me.

Sally started the account by explaining that the girl at the bric-a-brac stall had ignored her offer to buy the ornament, and she had eventually come to find me and ask me to try out my Dutch on the assistant to get the message over. She added that she had not come back with me to the stall, but had waited for the outcome of my bidding, at another booth.

"Now that I think back," I took up the tale, "the assistant did not seem too keen to serve me, and she only finalized the deal after looking at her watch. I thought she was in a hurry to get off duty, and decided to sell rather than have me keep her late for some appointment by bickering, and yet, that couldn't have been the reason," I frowned, "for she was still in the booth, aruging with the owner, when Sally and I passed by some ten minutes later."

"They could have been arguing over the fact that she had sold the dragon to the wrong person!" suggested Markheim. "Did you see anyone else at the stall?"

We both shook our heads.

Dirk interrupted.

"I wonder if the time factor had something to do with the sale? Sally says the girl ignored her offer to buy, and she didn't sell to Janey until she had made a time check. It is possible the identity of the buyer they were waiting for was not known to them. That it was a private deal, where no connection could be traced from one person to the next."

"A bit risky, surely, depending solely on the timing? What if several customers turned up at the same time?"

"They would have had to know what to ask for," said Sally, "and in this case, it was a chance in a million I spotted the dragon! It was lying among a heap of bric-a-bric on a tray in the shadows at the back of the booth. I happened to notice it because it was something I was looking for to add to my collection, and I only spotted it because I have very keen eyesight."

"And you specifically asked for the dragon?" asked Dirk, and we both nodded.

"That seems to explain it," agreed Markheim.

"It was rather an unfortunate coincidence for you."

"Never mind. Now that you know what was going on and have found the diamonds, and know that I haven't been up to anything nefarious, I can relax and enjoy my holiday without feeling I am being pursued all the time!"

I swallowed the last mouthful of coffee. "Can we go now?"

The Commissair eyed me thoughtfully, but ignored my plea.

"It would be interesting to find out who the diamonds were meant for, and who has been trailing around after you, and also," his voice hardened, "who it was that was indirectly responsible for the death of Vogel when he tried to escape from your room when he was surprised in his search there!"

"What do you mean?" I gasped.

"We found Vogel's prints on the furniture and inside the window of your bedroom, Miss Mathieson. This confirmed what we assumed—that since he was not wearing his outdoor clothes, entry to your room was made from inside the hotel. Our theory is that he was disturbed by the chambermaid, and dodged out onto the balcony to hide."

"The window was open when I went to fetch some snapshots during the evening." I frowned. "I shut it, and to make sure it wouldn't blow open again, I pushed some furniture against it. You don't think he was actually on the balcony while I was doing so, do you?"

"I doubt it. I think in the state he was in, the lad would panic and make a bid for the fire escape, without waiting to see who had come to the room. The chambermaid also made mention of an open window and a faulty catch when we questioned her."

There was a moment's silence, and Sally said impatiently, "Can we go now?"

"I was thinking." Again Markheim ignored the plea. "You might be able to help us further, Miss Mathieson. Whoever wants these diamonds thinks you still have the dragon in your possession. If you let it be known at the Collenius that you do have it in your bag, by, say, taking it out to show it off, a further attempt to get it will be made, without any doubt. This time, you will allow the attempt to succeed, and we shall be there, to tail the thief, in this instance probably your man with the scarred hands, to the person who is employing him to retrieve their property. It's the man behind this we want, not the small fry crooks he employs."

"But what about my bag? And my personal possessions!"

"Naturally we shall recover them for you."

"No, Janey!" said Mike firmly. "Don't get involved. You might get hurt."

He glared at Markheim and van der Woude.

"I don't suppose it has crossed your minds that Janey could be in danger if she helped you with this ploy? Or perhaps police work makes you so impersonal that you don't give a damn
180

what happens to your pawns so long as you can checkmate?"

A vein near van der Woude's temple dilated. I could see the quickening pulsation of his heartbeat as the blood throbbed through it, yet in spite of these symptoms of anger, his voice was cool when he replied.

"I would not have seconded this proposal if I had thought for a single moment that Janey might be in danger. When her bag gets snatched, she must let it go without a struggle, as though taken completely by surprise. My advice, however, is that she leaves it in a place from which it can easily be purloined, when she is having a coffee in the lounge, or dining out, or in a cocktail bar. The Commissair will have a man watching her all the time, so there will be no question of the bag and its contents not being returned to her in due course after the theft."

"Surely I would have to raise a hue and cry?" I pointed out.

"Naturally—but after a stunned silence. We want the man to have time to get away, or rather think he has got away with it."

"I would have to have my bag back without much delay," I decided. "I need what I carry in it."

Markheim hesitated. "You might be without it for a few hours."

"In that case," I decided, "I refuse to display the dragon blatantly for another twenty-four hours!"

"What do you mean?" barked Markheim.

"I came to The Hague to enjoy myself, not to do police work," I pointed out. "Already I have had most of this day ruined, when I might have been sightseeing. Tomorrow, I fully intend to go to Keukenhof and spend the day there.

"No," I repeated firmly. "Tomorrow night I shall cooperate with you, and flaunt the dragon in the lounge, but until then, no!"

"There could still be an attempt to steal the dragon from you, with or without your cooperation!" Dirk pointed out. "Since the article hasn't been found among the possessions you leave in your room, it will be presumed you must have it in your bag."

"In that case," I teased him, "you can act as my bodyguard at Keukenhof tomorrow! No one will guess that you are on official duty. You have been hanging around me so much," I tried not to let my bitterness show, "that whoever is watching me will have the mistaken idea that you have a personal interest in me!"

I stood up and looked down at them.

"Now, if you will excuse me, I am going back to the hotel. I am tired. I have had an exhausting two days and I could do with an early night."

I paused for a moment, looking directly at Dirk.

"If you decided to join us on our visit to Keukenhof tomorrow, Inspector van der Woude," I gritted my teeth over his name, "we intend to leave the Collenius about nine o'clock."

My glance moved to Markheim.

"I am sorry if you think that I am not being sufficiently cooperative." I drew a deep breath. "But surely another day won't make all that difference? After all, it was by the merest accident that you stumbled across the diamonds," I pointed out in a pleading tone.

Sally and Mike walked back towards the hotel with me. On our way, we went into the Hungarian restaurant in Old Molen Straat and lingered over a pleasant meal. In spite of the distraction of the gypsy violins and the bold-eyed violinist who came to serenade me, I was aware that Sally and Mike kept casting suspicious glances at everyone who came anywhere near us, and I felt like a prisoner out on special parole.

When we returned to the hotel, they both insisted in walking to the door of my bedroom with me and going into the room to make sure no one was lurking there and that the windows were securely shut, before they took their leave.

"You give me the creeps, the pair of you!" I forced a laugh. "No one is going to attack me!"

Mike wasn't in a laughing mood.

"In spite of van der Woude's suggestion that you are in no personal danger," he said, "I am not happy about the affair. That man you saw on the balcony of the Park Hotel could have been on his way from your room after rummaging through your cases. If you had wakened a few seconds earlier and discovered him in the room, you would have screamed, and heaven knows what might have happened!"

With these discomforting words ringing in my ears, I gave Sally and Mike a good night hug before closing the door behind them, turning the key in the lock, and shooting the extra bolt into position.

It was a persistent banging on my door which finally roused me the following morning from a deep, exhausted sleep. I stared with disbelief at the face of the alarm clock. It couldn't possibly be after nine o'clock! I sat up with a start.

"Janey! Janey! Are you all right?"

I recognized van der Woud's anxious voice as he called to me and banged urgently on the door once again.

I got out of bed, put on my flimsy dressing gown and crossed to the door.

"Of course I'm all right!" I mumbled, still only half awake as I unlocked the door. "I slept late! That's all!" I stifled a yawn as I peered at him through the few inches of open doorway. "Give me ten minutes and I shall be with you— that is," I added suspiciously, "if you have come to accompany me to Keukenhof?"

"I'll be generous and give you twenty!" The anxiety faded from his voice and there was an amused smile on his lips as he considered my sleep-flushed face and tousled hair. "I might even allow you to take some breakfast before we leave!"

If I hadn't known he was a policeman, on police duty, I would have thrilled to the pleasant banter. But I did know that even though he made light of the situation, I was not a special friend, only a special case, and this saddened me.

"I shall wait for you in the lobby beside the lift," he told me. "Sally and Mike are already having breakfast."

I closed the door and hurried to bathe and dress.

In spite of everything, today I wanted to look as if I hadn't a care in the world. I would pretend my official guardian angel was in fact a dear friend, and I would dress up for the occasion!

I decided to wear a favorite outfit—a cornflower-blue gabardine skirt with a blue silk shirt and short-sleeved cardigan, and I pinned a marcasite lizard brooch to the collar of my blouse and slipped a pearl and marcasite ring on to my finger. I tied my hair back with a long, chiffon cornflower-blue scarf.

Glancing in the mirror, I knew I was attractive-looking this morning, for my eyes were clear after the long, restful sleep, and the Dutch sun of the past days had given my cheeks a faint golden tan and intensified the golden streaks in my hair.

Oliver Saunders would have ogled me. Jan Stuyvesant would have paid me a heavy-handed compliment. Tim would have told me I looked not bad, and Dirk? I sighed to myself. Would he even notice what I looked like, or what I wore?

When I stepped from the lift I had to admit that he gave a very good impression of a young man delighted to see his girl of the moment, for although I could not see the expression in his eyes behind the dark glasses he was wearing today, he greeted me with a show of pleasure.

"You look lovely, Janey." He gave me an unexpected good-morning kiss on the cheek. "The flowers in the Keukenhof are going to hang their heads in envy!"

I blushed at his extravagant compliment.

"Don't be silly!" I retorted. "Whoever heard of tulips hanging their heads!"

"Keukenhof isn't only tulips," Dirk reminded me. "Although most of the hyacinths and daffodils are over, there are plenty of other bulbs and flowers to see!"

Dirk suggested we should pay a brief visit to Haarlem before going to Keukenhof. It was a delightful town with charming churches and on its outskirts the famous statue of Peter, the legendary boy who stuck his finger in the hole in the dyke to prevent the town from being flooded. On this occasion, it wasn't man's architecture or man's design in stone which fascinated me most. It was the gaiety of the little town, with garlands of flowers everywhere. They hung from the lamp standards, they clustered in baskets in the inns and shops, while flower pictures made up of tulip heads decorated the front lawns of the houses, and floats with fantastic floral designs moved through the streets. Even the barges on the canal were bedecked with flowers.

It was like walking through a floral fairy land, and I did not think anywhere else could measure up to this paradise, but then, I had not yet been to Keukenhof!

In the famous park, once the kitchen garden of the local castle, as the name signifies, I was dazzled by beauty.

The gardens were laid out formally, with paths and small lakes, where ducks swim happily in circles. Apart from the bulbs, here there were groves of flowering trees, and the blossom-heavy cherry trees and judas trees were set off against a natural backdrop of deeper-green woodland trees behind them. Everywhere, under the trees, there were drifts of color. It was almost impossible to put a finger between the clumps of flowers.

I was enchanted with the scene, the massed colors, the idyllic beauty of the setting. I forgot about mundane matters; forgot that Dirk was my official bodyguard and not the amusing friend he made an excellent pretense of being. I kept grabbing his arm to point out this and that to him, and gasped in wonder and delight at the sheer magnificence of the dazzling panorama.

I could have spent much longer simply looking at the flowers, but all too soon it was time to go.

"I think I would like to come back to Keukenhof every year at this time," I observed happily as Dirk opened the car door for me to get in.

"That would make your husband a Keukenhof widower!" he grinned. "I understand there are a few of them!"

He slipped into the back seat of the car beside me. "I wouldn't find it flattering to think my wife preferred looking at flowers to looking at me."

"That," said Sally, turning around to smile at him, "is because you are another of the male chauvinist clan! I'll bet there are more golf widows than Keukenhof widowers in the world!"

I said nothing. I had had a lovely day. I felt happy and relaxed and I had enjoyed the way Dirk paid attention to me. I liked the way he looked at me when he joined in the chorus of "Tulips from Amsterdam" which Mike and Sally were singing to each other in the front seat, and I even felt he had gone beyond the bounds of official duties when we stopped at a souvenir shop and he bought me a Delft tile, with a tulip design, because Delft blue was the color of my eyes.

I was happy and glowing with pleasure when we returned to the Collenius, but the glow quickly faded after Dirk went to phone Markheim to ask him if there had been any developments in our absence.

He came back to tell us the disconcerting news that the man with the scarred hands, a petty crook known to the local police, had been found drowned behind the wheel of his car, which had crashed into a canal at some time during the night.

*Chapter 15*

Mike asked Dirk when and where the accident had taken place, but van der Woude shook his head.

"I was given no details," he said, "merely told the fact, and asked to report to Markheim as soon as possible."

I tried not to look as miserable as I felt at this news, which meant that instead of dining with Mike, Sally and me in the Vermeer Room, Dirk would have to leave us straightaway.

He managed to look genuinely rueful about the change of plan, although all the time he was apologizing for having to leave us so unexpectedly, he kept glancing impatiently at his watch, as if wondering just how quickly he could rush off without appearing impolite.

Sally and I went to the reception desk to get our room keys, and when the receptionist handed them over, she also handed us a colorful piece of pasteboard, which turned out to be a free ticket for a show at the HOT Theater the following evening. Attached to the tickets was a typed "With Compliments" slip from the tour group which had arranged our trip, and I noticed that similar tickets were sticking out from other pigeonholes behind the desk.

Before dining, we went to the cocktail bar for an apéritif. Sally and I wriggled on to the tall bar stools, and Mike stood beside us and asked what we wanted to drink.

I opened my bag to get change to pay for the Cinzano I ordered, just as Oliver Saunders came weaving his way toward us. He was rather unsteady on his feet, and as he came up to me he tripped over the leg of the stool. He made a wild grab at the counter to stop himself from falling, didn't quite make it, and caught hold of me instead, knocking my bag from my hand and sending the contents scattering in all directions.

I was furious, particularly since Oliver continued to cling to my waist with his clammy hands, and I pushed him away and told him to pick up the bits and pieces, if he was capable of so doing!

He gave a silly titter, bent down and picked up the dragon which was lying at his feet, and waving it gaily in the air for all to see, he solemnly proclaimed that he was St. George and I was the damsel he was going to rescue from the horrendous beast!

Most of the people around us were laughing at his antics, but Mike and Sally, their faces showing patent annoyance with his nonsense, stooped down to help me retrieve my belongings, which I stuffed higgledy-piggledy back into my bag.

I made an attempt to get the dragon from Oliver, but he kept tittering drunkenly and passing it from one hand to the other, as I tried to take it from him.

I looked around for his usual companions, hoping they would come and take their drunken friend away. They were sitting at a table in the far corner of the room, watching what was happening, but making no effort to take their leading man under their wing.

Eventually Mike managed to pinion his waving arms and I was able to retrieve the ornament, in spite of Oliver's weepy protests that it was now his since he had killed it.

The unfortunate scene quite spoiled the evening for us. We hastily finished our drinks and left the bar, and instead of dining in the hotel as originally planned, we walked down the road to a small Italian restaurant, where we sat for a time eating spaghetti and chatting, reminiscing about Tim's wedding and the events of the day.

We were all three sleepy after the long day in the open air, and decided to go to bed early, hoping, as we returned to the Collenius, that we would not have the misfortune to run into Saunders again, especially if he had had more to drink since the last time we had seen him.

Van der Woude telephoned me shortly after eight o'clock the next morning to tell me that he had been told of the incident with Oliver in the cocktail bar, and that he was coming around to talk to me about it over breakfast, if that was convenient.

I smiled ruefully to myself. As far as I was concerned, any time was a convenient time for me to see him. We arranged to meet in the breakfast room at nine o'clock, and it was exactly on the stroke of the hour that we met there and over several cups of coffee discussed the incident.

I was quite sure Oliver's actions had been accidental. I was equally sure that everyone in the cocktail bar, and in the lounge beyond, had seen the dragon which he had been waving aloft.

Dirk eyed me gravely.

"Any time at all now, Janey," he warned me, "you can expect another attempt to get hold of it. Remember," he gave a cautionary shake of the head, "this time when someone grabs for your bag, let the thief get away with it."

I shivered uneasily.

"It's horrible, this feeling of being a marked woman! I hate the idea of being waylaid and robbed."

"Don't worry, my dear. We shall be keeping a very watchful eye on you, to make sure your belongings are only removed temporarily from your safekeeping." Dirk gave me a reassuring smile. "You have nothing to worry about, unless—" He looked at me thoughtfully.

"Yes?"

"You are lunching with Stuyvesant today, aren't you?"

I nodded.

"Then try to see to it that if an attempt occurs when he is with you, he doesn't try any heroics."

I grinned.

"I think the heroics would be in the enemy camp, if anyone tried to snatch my bag with Jan in the offing. I don't think anyone would be so foolhardy."

I was right. I spent a peaceful, amiable few hours in Jan's company. He arrived at the hotel shortly after eleven, to take me to the Mauritshuis which he knew I was keen to visit. While I stared with pleasure at Vermeer's lovely "View of Delft" and his equally appealing "Head of a Girl,' Jan, true to form, stood entranced in front of Paulus Potter's famous painting of a young bull.

We lunched in the Copper Kettle grill room of Des Indes Hotel, and over lunch, finding me a sympathetic audience, Jan told me about the girl he had loved and left behind in Vermont.

"She loves her own country so very much, Janey, I could not ask her to come and live here, in Holland. It is so very different there from here!"

"Jan!" I stared at him. "Do you mean to tell me you love this girl, but you haven't told her so? You haven't asked her to marry you?"

"I didn't want to hear her say no!" he replied unhappily. "What could I give her to make up for what she would be leaving behind?"

"Jan Stuyvesant, either you are a coward or the shyest man I have ever met, in spite of your hearty, hail-fellow-well-met manner! Listen to me!" I commanded. "The only way a girl can tell if she is loved is when a man tells her so and asks her to marry him. You told me that your Lisa seemed quite upset when you were leaving, isn't that so?"

He nodded.

"Then, if you have an ounce of sense in you, before someone else catches her on the rebound, you go home this afternoon and telephone her. Tell her how wonderful she is. Tell her you want to marry her! I have an idea you will get the answer you want, but if you don't, you are no worse off. If you do," I smiled, "tell her you are flying out on the first available flight to ask her father's consent."

Jan eyed me keenly.

"As a woman, this is what you think would be the best thing to do?"

"Try it and see, Jan!" I egged him on. "She would be a fool to turn you down just because your home is here in Holland! I think you are very nice myself, Jan!" I teased him laughingly.

After the advice I gave him, Jan couldn't wait to get home and carry it out. He drove me back to the Collenius, grinning like a schoolboy all the way, and left me there to kick my heels idly in the hotel for the rest of the afternoon, while he broke the speed record for the journey from The Hague to Leeuwarden.

In spite of the sunshine, I did not feel like going for a stroll through the town on my own, nor did I consider loitering in the pretty park behind the hotel.

The thought that someone might be lurking near me, waiting for an opportunity to snatch my bag from me, made me nervous, even though Dirk had assured me that there would be someone to keep an eye on me at all times.

I was delighted when Sally and Mike returned from their visit to the miniature town of Madurodam in time for us to enjoy a late afternoon coffee together, and I was even more delighted when Dirk joined us in the evening for a *Rijstafel* at Woo Ping's, the Indonesian restaurant to which Tim had hoped to take us on our first night in The Hague.

In spite of our fears, or possibly hopes in the case of the police, no one made any attempt to snatch my bag from me. No one, apart from the men who were on official duty, lurked in the shadows watching me. No one tried to sneak into my bedroom.

The inaction was as discomforting as the expected action. Mike drew his own conclusions from it, although Dirk disagreed with his findings.

Mike was certain that the man with the scarred hands had been the major figure in the robbery attempts, and now that he was dead, the case was closed. Whoever had parted with the diamonds doubtless thought they had reached their correct destination and wouldn't be worrying about them, so there would be no more trouble.

Dirk's idea, which was shared by Markheim, was that the diamonds had been a bribe, discreetly passed on to someone for benefits received. Since they had not been reported as stolen, this was the most obvious conclusion to reach.

"It is the way the corruption game is played nowadays," explained Dirk. "Both parties are most discreet, since the penalties can be heavy, and they take great pains to cover their tracks so that the currency of the bribe can be traced to neither one nor the other. In one instance I know of, a man picked up a tatty-looking painting at an antique shop. He paid a modest sum for it, and it was recorded as a legitimate sale. Oddly, it turned out to be a genuine Picasso, and he made a mint from it, while the man who had arranged for him to have it made an even larger fortune from the contract he landed. Nothing could be proved. There are so many Picassos on the market, it is impossible to say to whom this or that one belonged!"

"And you think the diamonds come into the same sort of deal?" I asked.

"We are certain of it. Muller, the man who died in the car accident, was too small fry to be in possession of such a fortune. No," he said harshly, "we are sure he was merely employed to retrieve the dragon, and now that he is dead, someone else will be asked to do the job. No one would let a fortune like that slip through their fingers!"

Yet, in spite of his words, Wednesday morning and afternoon went past without incident, and the hours passed pleasantly for me, since van der

Woude appeared to have appointed himself my official companion. We strolled around the town together and talked and laughed together, and if we didn't hold hands and gaze rapturously into each other's eyes, as Mike and Sally did as they trailed after us, what did it matter?

In the evening, Oliver Saunders, who had been peeved with me because I had turned down the trip to Bussum, insisted that the least I could do to make up for his disappointment was to let him join our party on our visit to the late night show at the HOT Theater. He tagged along with us, but to our relief he met up with a girl he knew in the theater, and left us to go off with her.

It was very late when the show finished. In spite of Dirk's presence, I didn't look forward to the longish walk back to the hotel through the dark and empty streets. Sally and Mike walked ahead of us, arms around each other's waist, and Dirk amiably followed suit.

We had reached a particularly dark and lonely part of the road when three motor bikes came zooming toward us. They skidded to a halt within a couple of feet from us, then tried to scare us by driving around and around us in ever narrowing circles.

"Ignore them!" Dirk told me. "It's a game the local Hell's Angels play with pedestrians late at night. They soon buzz off."

He was wrong. Like sheepdogs shepherding sheep in different directions the bikes zoomed around and around, separating Mike and Sally from Dirk and me, and then, when I instinctively jumped to the side as one of them brushed against me, they managed to force Dirk and me apart. With their frightening tactics they kept chasing me further and further from my friends, until I was several yards away from them and forced to retreat into an alleyway where a car, with its engine running, was parked.

I tried to dodge away from the bike which was pursuing me, but the driver kept circling nearer and nearer, until my back was hard against the side of the car. Next moment, a hand was thrust through the open window of the car, and I felt a tug on my arm as it grabbed at my bag.

Instinctively, forgetful of Dirk's warning, I clung on to it. The hand continued to tug the bag, pulling me around, and I found myself staring at a grotesque face in a nylon stocking mask. The nylon had laddered over the left ear, and through the hole I glimpsed a diamond-studded, crescent-shaped earring which I recognized immediately.

"Natasha!" The word rose in a whisper to my lips.

With an angry oath the woman released her grip of the bag and abruptly flung open the car door, so that I was knocked to the ground, almost under the wheels of the circling bike.

As I lay gasping for breath, Natasha sent the car rocketing forward, turned it in a tight circle which made the tires scream in protest, and came racing back directly toward where I was lying.

The lads on the motor bikes, realizing what she intended to do, and wanting no part of it, went zooming out of sight, and Dirk, sprinting towards me, shouted my name.

I managed to scramble to my feet, but the car was now only yards away, and I was too shaken to move quickly.

I let out a scream of hopeless terror as Dirk launched himself forward in a rugby tackle and somehow managed to push me out of harm's way as the wing of the car caught his shoulder and sent him flying.

We both got to our feet again, but Natasha hadn't finished with us. She sent the car into another screeching turn and drove at us again.

Dirk grabbed my arm, pulled me toward the railing which protected a shop entrance, then looked for a way of escape as the car continued to race toward us, faster and faster, snarling with power like an animal gone berserk.

With only seconds to spare we leaped out of its path, to be showered with glass as it ploughed through the railing, into the entrance-way and then up against the glass door of the shop. There it came to rest, its horn raising a continuous protest as Natasha remained slumped across the steering wheel.

People came from all directions to find out what was going on. Police and an ambulance arrived. Dirk escorted me to a police car and told the driver to take me to the Collenius. He told me brusquely he would be in touch later and with a brisk, official salute, he walked away.

## Chapter 16

Natasha died in hospital later that night, but
before she died she made a statement to the police. Dirk telephoned me at midnight to tell me
the story.

Natasha had been a compulsive gambler. For
months she had been up to the eyes in debt to
various bookmakers, who were dunning her for
money and threatening to go to her husband.

Berg had known of his wife's failing, but she
had sworn to him that she had given up gam-
bling when they married. In order that she
would not be tempted to revert to her old habits,
he gave her almost everything she asked for—
model clothes, fast cars, jewelry, furs, backing
for the plays she wanted to appear in—but
never actual cash for spending. She could not
sell her jewelry to pay off her debts, because
each piece was insured and he checked her collection regularly.

She had been at her wits' end what to do,
when she was approached by the head of a large
engineering firm which was tendering for a five-

million-dollar contract to build a new deep-water harbor and dam. This man knew that in most respects Natasha could get her husband to do anything she wanted. He had also learned about her debts, and he offered to give her uncut diamonds to the value of £30,000, a sum far beyond her dreams actually to possess, if she persuaded her husband to put the contract his way. The deal would be done discreetly. The stones, hidden in the dragon for ease in smuggling back to Britian, would be left with a middleman, who would sell the ornament to the customer who came to his stall at a given time and asked specifically for it.

All would have gone well if Natasha's watch hadn't been five minutes slow, and if I hadn't turned up at the precise time arranged and asked for the dragon.

When Natasha turned up and found it had been sold, both she and the stallholder tried to recover it from me, for the assistant had given them an accurate description of the woman who had bought it.

Much of what happened after this I knew, except for the fact that it had been Natasha who had arranged the tickets for the HOT Theater, and, confirming that I was going to the performance, she had also arranged an ambush for me on my way home after the show by instructing the three young hoodlums on the motorbikes to get me separated from my friends and herded in her direction.

Again her plans miscarried. She didn't get the

bag, I recognized her, and in a fit of recklessness, seeing no other way to prevent me from giving her away, she tried to kill me.

"I thought you would like to know the whole story before you went to bed, Janey," Dirk concluded. "You will also be glad to know that the police are no longer interested in you. The case of the diamond dragon is closed, and you can go to sleep with a tranquil mind.

"Goodnight, my dear. It was nice knowing you, and I wish you bon voyage for tomorrow!"

Before I could reply, he put down the receiver.

I stared blindly at the telephone I still held in my hand, before replacing it on its cradle. So that was that as far as Dirk was concerned. It was all over. The case was finished. I had meant nothing personal to him. I had merely been someone he had met in the course of his work; a pretty girl it had been his duty to keep his eye on for a few days.

Somehow I could not leave it at that. I telephoned the hospital in the morning, on the pretext of asking how he was, but I was told he had left.

I waited, hoping against hope for a phone call. None came. I looked for him in the breakfast room, for he knew the time we were leaving, but he was not there.

Now I knew for a certainty that I had been only a brief episode in his life. A part of yesterday, but not tomorrow.

Mike drove Sally and me to the airport. I

tried to take part in their cheerful conversation, but my heart wasn't in it and eventually I lapsed into silence.

Sally and Mike didn't notice. They were too wrapped up in themselves, and when they fell silent, it was because they didn't need to talk to one another. The way they smiled at each other was more expressive than words.

I envied them their absorption with each other and the happiness they found in each other's company. I envied all lovers. If only Dirk had telephoned before I left the hotel, to say he was sorry I was leaving, that it hadn't merely been in the line of duty he had taken me out and about, and flirted with me, and chaffed me, and one occasion, boldly kissed me, I would have been able to look back on my Dutch holiday with a happier heart. What saddened me so much was that it had all been play-acting.

The trees which lined the motorway thinned out, and I caught sight of pleasant farms, placid cows and a giant windmill, its blades standing out clearly against the blue of the sky. Then came the tulip fields spreading out their carpets of gold and pink and red across the flat landscape, and I could not bear to look at them because they reminded me of Dirk. I could almost feel his presence beside me, hear his pleasant tenor voice as he sang "Tulips from Amsterdam," and see his eyes twinkle at me as if he meant the words specially for me.

Tears pricked my eyelids. How he would have laughed if he had seen my handbag today, stuffed to an even bulkier shape because inside it was the carefully wrapped blue tile he had given me as a souvenir, and the box of liqueur chocolates he had purchased in the shop near the hotel to try to get even with Mike, who had brought chocolates last night for Sally to take with her on our visit to the HOT Theater.

A silly song went buzzing around and around in my head: "Memories are Made of This."

I had memories. Memories of a man standing in the rain, chatting me up beside a chess stall under the lime trees of the Lange Voorhout. Memories of a man playing baseball with young children among the sand dunes at Scheveningen. Memories of a man who could be tender and gentle, strong and angry. Memories of a long good night kiss. Memories of a man who had shouted a frantic warning to me, and saved my life, and then walked out of it, to leave me to be comforted by strangers.

I sighed aloud and Mike looked up into his driving mirror, caught my eyes and smiled.

"Cheer up, Janey! The end of a holiday isn't the end of the world, is it, Sally?" He looked at the girl by his side, and again I felt a stab of envy.

This wasn't the end for them, only the beginning.

He stopped at the entrance of the airport building so that Sally and I could get out with our luggage, and drove off to find a space in the car park.

"Janey! Don't look so down in the mouth!"

Sally chided me. "I know it wasn't the kind of holiday we anticipated, but it had its moments, and here comes one of them." She giggled.

I looked around with a hopeful start, but it was Jan Stuyvesant who came striding toward us, grinning from ear to ear. He gave us both a resounding kiss, and Mike, hurrying along the pavement behind him called out, "Hey! That's my girl your flirting with!"

"I love everybody today!" Jan said jubilantly, picking up all our cases as if they were matchbox-light and striding ahead of us into the departure hall to find the notice board which gave information about flight times.

He dumped the luggage down beside it and looked at me with another joyous grin.

"Janey, apart from one other very special person, you are the most wonderful girl in the world!"

He turned to the other two. "She gave me a piece of very good advice, you know! She told me to telephone Vermont. Not to wait another day, but to do it pronto, and tell the girl I left back there that I loved her and am going to fly out next week to tell her so in person and ask her to marry me! And guess what?" I thought his lips would crack with the breadth of his smile as he continued. "She said 'Yes'!"

"Jan! I am so glad!" I gave him a hug.

"Me too!" Sally stood on tiptoe to kiss him.

"Do you mind if I join in the queue for kisses?"

I swung around.

205

Dirk van der Woude had come quietly up behind us. He looked pale. His smile wavered, and he kept one arm stiffly behind his back.

"Dirk!" I could not keep the lilting gladness from my voice nor could I hide the happiness in my eyes.

"Dirk! You came! I thought—"

"Yes?"

"I phoned the hospital this morning and they said you had left. I thought," I sniffed with remembered misery, "I thought I wasn't going to see you ever again!"

As far as we were concerned, no one else in the teeming airport existed. We stood there, grinning stupidly at each other, not quite sure of ourselves, not quite believing what was happening.

"Janey, surely you knew I wouldn't let you go without a goodbye kiss!" His voice trembled.

"Last night you walked away from me!" I accused him.

"Last night I wasn't myself. I was shocked by what nearly happened to you. Shocked to find out just how much you meant to me. Afraid I might give my feelings away and have you reject me. You had said you had had enough of policemen!

"Then this morning," his eyes began to twinkle, "I thought again. I remembered the way you looked at me as I turned away from you. There had been an appeal in your eyes. A look which could have been tenderness. So this morning," he repeated, "I had second thoughts and so I came here to give you a farewell present. Only," he was grinning stupidly, "I don't think I can bear to part with it, because it reminds me so much of a girl I would like to know better!"

He took his hand from behind his back and stiffly held out the blue-eyed doll in the gingham dress. The doll I had wanted to buy that day which seemed so long ago; the doll he had said then reminded him of me; the doll he had bought on the spur of the moment, hoping one day to give to me.

I took it and held it, and I was half laughing, half crying as I looked at him.

"Dirk! Oh, Dirk! You idiot!"

A disembodied voice announced the departure time of the flight Sally and I were booked on, but I didn't hear the words. I wasn't paying attention to anyone but Dirk, and the way he was looking at me, which lifted me high in the sky of happiness.

I had liked him from the moment we had met. I had found him more attractive than any man I had hitherto met. There had even been times, this past day, when I had hated him. Now, however, gazing at him, smiling at his smile, feeling the warmth of happiness flood through me as he held out his arms for a goodbye-till-we-meet-again embrace, I knew what these emotions added up to.

Suddenly, I knew I was in love!